A COMMON BOND

She'd be the first to admit she'd been away a long time. She didn't expect to recognize every face. But she was sure this man wasn't anyone she'd ever known.

She studied him surreptitiously. His thick dark hair was swept off his face in a neat, contemporary style, but Jenny got the impression that this was his only concession to fashion. It wasn't that he didn't dress well. There was just something about him that marked him as different. She guessed that he was a maverick, deliciously uncivilized, and much too exciting for this sleepy town. He didn't belong on a little island off the coast of Oregon any more that she did.

Dear Reader,

Welcome to Silhouette! Our goal is to give you hours of unbeatable reading pleasure, and we hope you'll enjoy each month's six new Silhouette Desires. These sensual, provocative love stories are both believable and compelling—sometimes they're poignant, sometimes humorous, but always enjoyable.

Indulge yourself. Experience all the passion and excitement of falling in love along with our heroine as she meets the irresistible man of her dreams and together they overcome all obstacles in the path to a happy ending.

If this is your first Desire, I hope it'll be the first of many. If you're already a Silhouette Desire reader, thanks for your support! Look for some of your favorite authors in the coming months: Stephanie James, Diana Palmer, Dixie Browning, Ann Major and Doreen Owens Malek, to name just a few.

Happy reading!

Isabel Swift
Senior Editor

SDRL-7/85

BEVERLY BIRD
All the Marbles

Silhouette Desire

Published by Silhouette Books New York

America's Publisher of Contemporary Romance

SILHOUETTE BOOKS
300 E. 42nd St., New York, N.Y. 10017

Copyright © 1985 by Beverly Bird

Distributed by Pocket Books

ISBN: 0-373-05227-8

First Silhouette Books printing August, 1985

10 9 8 7 6 5 4 3 2 1

America's Publishers of Contemporary Romance

Printed in the U.S.A.

BEVERLY BIRD

currently makes her home in Arizona, though she spent most of her life on a small island off the coast of New Jersey. She is devoted to both her husband and her writing, but still makes time for travel and horseback riding.

For Steve, for the perseverance that made the year—and the marbles—possible.

1

She'd be the first to admit that she'd been away a long time. She didn't expect to recognize and remember every face. Yet she was sure that this man wasn't anyone she'd ever met.

Jenny Oliver's interest quickened as she watched the stranger follow her onto the elevator and plant himself squarely in the middle of it. Eventually, a wry grin touched her mouth. Whoever he was, she thought, he had to be better entertainment than thinking about the horrors that had greeted her when she had returned to Little Beach that morning. As the old elevator groaned its way upward she studied him surreptitiously, temporarily forgetting the other man who had been haunting her thoughts all morning . . . a man whose name she didn't know and whose face she'd never seen. That man held one very large monkey wrench and could easily drop it into her plans. This man seemed infinitely more appealing to contemplate.

He was tall, but more than that, he looked tough and sinewy. His thick, dark hair was swept back off his face in a neat, contemporary style, but Jenny got the impression that this was his one and only concession to fashion. It wasn't that he wasn't dressed well; his jeans, snakeskin boots, and gray sport jacket were acceptable enough, although she felt sure that he wore them more to please himself than anyone else. There was just something about him that went deeper than the clothes he wore, something that marked him as different. He didn't belong on this sleepy little island off the southern coast of Oregon any more than she did. She guessed that he was a maverick, somehow deliciously uncivilized and much too exciting for this sleepy, tiny town.

There were ever so slight age lines around his mouth and eyes. They made him look jaded and inexplicably sexy. She decided that his eyes looked as though they had seen too much hard living—and probably quite a bit of hard loving. Another dead giveaway that he hadn't been born and raised in Little Beach, Jenny thought. The people here didn't do anything hard. They met each day with a simple "what will be, will be" acceptance that she found both admirable and irritating.

The elevator lurched to a stop and the door creaked open again. Jenny had been so lost in her perusal of the man who stood beside her that the movement startled her. She crashed back to reality with disorienting speed and a comical sound of surprise.

It was then that the stranger finally turned to look at her. The eyes that she had imagined as romantically jaded were shrewd yet somehow expressionless, reminding her of two shiny black stones. Jenny left the car hurriedly, feeling oddly let down.

It didn't seem unusual to her that he left the elevator as well. The fifth and top floor of Timber House—the ramshackle old inn that had been in her family for generations—housed more than just the offices of the hotel staff. The Olivers had traditionally rented out any spare rooms there to local merchants and businessmen. Jenny assumed that the stranger was headed for one of those.

Until she reached the end of the corridor and he was still following her silently.

A strange mixture of excitement and alarm knotted inside her. There were only two doors at this end of the corridor. One opened onto stairs leading up to a widow's walk that her great-grandfather had added in 1902. The other opened onto her father's office—now, by a cruel twist of fate, her own. Jenny had a hard time believing that the man was headed for the widow's walk. It had obviously gone unused during all the years she had been away—that much had been evidenced by the fact that she'd had to break through several old, rusty locks in order to get up there earlier that morning. She couldn't imagine that anyone other than herself would want to fight the cobwebs and precariously antique stairs to go up there. In which case, she thought, it was probably safe to assume that this stranger was going to her office.

He *was* following her. But why?

Jenny glanced over her shoulder at him, her gray eyes wary now. This time, sharp surprise registered on the man's chiseled features as she caught his gaze. It was as though he were seeing her for the first time. His eyes raked over her quickly and assessingly, then flicked to the door of her father's office as though to verify something. Finally, his face closed beneath a neutral mask. He met her eyes steadily but still said nothing.

A strange chill touched Jenny's skin, as though someone had left a window open to the cool, damp Pacific air. She didn't know him, but she was equally sure that he *did* know her—and that he was following her for a reason. It was eerie, it made no sense, but she knew that she was right. A wave of pure apprehension swept away the last of her excitement.

Her response was instinctive. On a purely logical level, she didn't truly believe that the man meant her any harm. But then, it hadn't been a purely logical morning. Her nerves and emotions were tangled and close to the surface, and she reacted with almost primitive impulsiveness. She reached quickly for the doorknob, stepped into her office, then started to close the door again.

The stranger blocked it with his foot.

Startled—she'd been hoping against hope that her imagination was running away with her, that this wasn't really happening—Jenny pulled the door open a crack to confront him. Her sooty eyes were wide, her throat tight.

"What do you think you're doing?" she managed to ask. Her voice was a soft croak that struggled valiantly for strength. It had been a long, nerve-wracking day, and it was only half over. A stranger stalking her in the corridor was something she really didn't need.

The man's raven eyes roamed over her speculatively again, and she had to wonder for a moment if he was going to answer her. He seemed more intent on scrutinizing the burnished, dark gold mane of her hair—windblown now from her visit to the widow's walk earlier—and the wrinkled remains of what had once been her favorite blue linen slacks. Then his eyes finally snapped back to hers and he responded, "It would seem that I'm here to see you."

His voice was rusty and low, but held a contradictory tinge of an East Coast accent. Jenny blinked at him in surprise. "Me?" she echoed. "Whatever for?"

He didn't bother to answer either question. Instead, he countered with one of his own. "Where did you think I was going? The next office down?"

His voice was mocking. A sardonic smile touched his lips as he reached out to push the door open again. Jenny flushed. It was obvious that he knew as well as she did that there was no next office down.

She stepped back out of the doorway quickly, instinctively putting distance between them as he started to move past her into the office. He sauntered to the center of the room with a quelling yet somehow indifferent air of authority. She hesitated a moment, then followed him.

"Well, if you're looking for me, then I suppose you might as well come in and introduce yourself," she answered belatedly, trying to regain some semblance of the upper hand. This was, after all, her hotel now. As absurd as it seemed to her at the moment, she was still in charge.

She didn't offer any explanation for her behavior as she followed him into the office. If hers had been odd, she thought, then his had been frightening and deliberately provoking. He might have said something to her in the elevator instead of playing out some great cloak-and-dagger routine and scaring her half to death. She cast him a dark look, then moved around behind her desk and sat down with deliberate dignity.

"Well?" she prodded him, her annoyance making her voice cool.

The man lowered his lean, hard-looking frame onto a nearby sofa. Then, instead of answering her, his dark eyes roamed over the office. It looked bare without Ed's plethora of nautical antiques, and when his eyes finally came back to her, Jenny thought she detected a faint shadow of sorrow in his nearly unfathomable gaze.

Then it faded, and his broad shoulders grew rigid. She decided immediately that she had been mistaken. "You've taken all of Ed's stuff out of here," he observed. His voice was still rusty, but now there was a hint of accusation in it. "You move pretty fast for someone who didn't even get here in time for the funeral."

Jenny's eyes widened in surprise. "He—he was my father," she began shakily. "I have the right to mourn him as I choose."

"You don't choose to attend funerals?" he prodded her further, his voice dangerously idle as he continued to look around the room.

Jenny's eyes widened even more in utter disbelief. She stared at him speechlessly. Then, gradually, anger surfaced to replace her shock. "I wasn't invited!" she responded in a clipped voice. "The only choice I had when it came to how I was going to mourn Ed Oliver concerned his possessions. I packed them up and took them home. I'm not going to make a shrine out of his office, if that's what you're suggesting. He wouldn't have wanted one. He was a practical, unemotional man. Not that it's any business of yours. Who are you?"

A faint thread of hysteria tangled with her voice as she finished despite all of her best efforts to keep it smooth. Just before she ducked her head quickly in an effort to control herself, she thought she saw another flicker of emotion in those obsidian eyes. What? Sorrow again? Sympathy? By the time she looked up again, it was too late to tell.

The man got to his feet and approached her desk with such deliberate intent that she had to wonder what he planned to do once he reached it. She fought against the urge to cringe. He seemed to be such a powerful man, and she couldn't forget her first clear impression of him in the elevator—that he was somehow untamed. That, and residual panic from having been so artfully stalked down the corridor, made her pull back in her chair warily as he extended his hand to her.

"Let's just say that I was a friend of your father's. My name is Gage Pierce," he drawled in the same low voice. Jenny forced herself to meet his gaze straight on as she took his hand. His palm was unexpectedly warm and dry, and there was an inherent strength in his grip that was vaguely comforting after the horrendous morning she had had. She stiffened in surprise. She had expected his touch to be as remote as his demeanor.

"Pleased to meet you," she managed to say, carefully disengaging her hand from his. His touch made her feel more than a little uncomfortable. She'd felt the wildest urge to jump as they had made contact, and she wasn't normally a jittery person.

"Unfortunately," she went on, regaining her composure, "a name doesn't count for much in these parts, Mr. Pierce. Around here, you've got to be someone's nephew or cousin. Now, *that's* an introduction, and it'll get you through any door on the island just like that." She snapped her fingers for emphasis, forcing a small, wry smile to her lips.

And then she caught his eyes. For a brief moment, she considered the possibility that the man she'd thought she'd seen in the elevator really did exist, and that he might laugh at her apt description of social distinction in Little Beach. She was wrong. He only lifted an eyebrow at her sardonically and returned to the sofa. He hooked one strong leg over the other and slung an arm over the back of the cushions, his eyes never leaving her. Jenny watched the process as though mesmerized, once again sensing a subdued but wild power in him. It took all the willpower she possessed to ignore the sudden fluttering of her heart and wrench her eyes back to his face as he spoke.

"I told you that I was a friend of your father's," he reminded her in an even tone of voice that effectively made her feel ridiculous for having forgotten that. Ridiculous . . . and vulnerable. His hard, male presence and the watchfulness of his dark eyes made her feel more unsure of herself than she had all morning, despite the chaos with which she had had to cope. Was it any wonder that she was having trouble keeping up with the conversation?

Still, she rallied quickly. "Not good enough," she said, bouncing back. "A lot of men have called themselves Ed Oliver's friends. He didn't agree with all that many of them."

"So you still want my references," he supplied. His voice was as even as before, revealing nothing. It made his question sound somehow dangerous.

Jenny only met his dark eyes guardedly and nodded.

"In terms of nephews and cousins?"

"This is the original Smalltown, U.S.A., Mr. Pierce. Familial connections are everything. I might, however, be persuaded to forgo the relatives and settle for learning the purpose of your visit. I don't live here any longer. I can afford to be generous when it comes to guarding the town gates against strangers." As she spoke, she relaxed in her chair with a satisfied sigh. For the first time since he'd blocked the door with his foot, she'd sounded strong and capable, fully in possession of the upper hand . . . if only for a moment.

Suddenly, his eyes snared hers in a look of silent challenge. Jenny felt a shiver tickle down her spine. She knew virtually nothing about this man, and yet she knew that something charged and very important was taking place between them. Their eyes held, but he wasn't just watching her. He was waiting. But for what? For her to do or say something that would enable him to size her up more fully? Because that was what he was doing. He was sizing her up, weighing her, just as he had done in the corridor. She knew that as clearly as if he had said so. He expected something of her; she simply couldn't figure out why or what.

She licked her lips nervously and forced herself to hold his eyes. Somehow, she won the wordless battle. He spoke first.

"I take it that you're an expert on Little Beach?" he asked eventually. In spite of her determination not to, Jenny started slightly at the rough assessment she sensed in his voice. He

13

hadn't given up. He was still trying to weigh her, and it bothered her more than she cared to admit that she couldn't tell what sort of scale he was using.

"I should be," she answered cautiously. "I lived here for twenty long years."

"But not the last nine," he supplied.

Her gray eyes narrowed suspiciously. "No," she responded slowly, drawing the word out as she tried to figure out what he was up to. "Not the last nine."

"Then perhaps I should be questioning you about *your* purpose," he suggested drily. "I've been living here for five years. If anyone's going to guard Little Beach's gates against outsiders, it should be me."

"You?" she repeated, feeling vulnerable again. She understood suddenly that while she might win a battle or two with this man, she would never win the war. He was a strong man, accustomed to being in charge.

"I'm not anyone's cousin or nephew," he went on, "but the people around here seem to have accepted me well enough. Including your father. In fact, I'd go so far as to say that he went one better than accepting me. He needed me. He also died three days ago, and now I find a stranger in his private office. So I suppose I should be asking you what you're up to. You see, I *was* his friend. I helped him when no one else would . . . or could," he allowed as an afterthought.

Another premonitory shiver shook Jenny. He knew she wasn't a stranger. He knew she was Ed's daughter. He was trying to make a point, and she thought she knew what it was.

"Ed needed you?" she asked carefully, unwilling to believe what she was coming to suspect. "What are you trying to tell me?"

Instead of answering, he got to his feet again and pulled an envelope from the pocket of his sport jacket. He crossed to her and dropped it on her desk casually—too casually.

Jenny stared down at it as though it were some sort of reptile. Alarm crawled through her. "What's this?"

"Proof," Gage answered. "I guessed I'd need it."

She glanced up at him quickly before turning her attention

back to the envelope. "Proof of what?" she asked. Silly question, she thought. She knew. There was no doubt in her mind. Yet she had a perverse desire to hear the words spoken aloud.

He sat on the edge of her desk, crossing his arms over his chest as he watched her. "Proof of our partnership," he answered eventually. "You know, when two separate persons both own half of a given establishment. Like this hotel, for instance."

"Like this hotel," she repeated hollowly, still staring at the envelope.

Surprise flickered briefly in Gage's obsidian eyes. He hadn't expected such a dull response from her—already he was learning that she could give as good as she got. Now, as he watched her, he was forced to admit that he hadn't been prepared for that. He'd anticipated finding a much different woman in Ed's office today. On some level, he'd expected her to be as cold and as untouchable as fine china. Another Abby, perhaps; a woman whose touch turned objects to ice. Everything he knew about her enforced such expectations. She hadn't made it back to Little Beach for her father's funeral. She hadn't made it back to Little Beach in nearly ten years, despite the fact that her father had been sick, despite the fact that he'd needed her. She alone had had the talent to rescue the old man's dying dream . . . and she had used that talent to promote a stranger's interest rather than his. She *should* have been cold, perfect, a mannequin of a woman.

Instead, she was as windblown, nervous, and wildly beautiful as a colt turned out to pasture for the first time. She could pause in regal, wary stillness or launch into flight without warning. And she had eyes as hot as silver fire. Sometimes. Now those eyes were lifeless and resigned. He found the change disconcerting and oddly disturbing. He found *her* disturbing. She was plucking at a sense of wonder deep inside him that he would have preferred to have seen gone untouched. Because she wasn't what Ed had—intentionally or not—led him to expect? Or because she was so . . . alive?

He shook his head almost imperceptibly as though to get rid of the nagging thoughts, then watched her critically as she reached slowly across the desk. Jenny was unaware of his perusal now. In truth, she knew exactly what she would find inside the envelope, and that was all she could think about. A nightmare had erupted upon her return to Little Beach that morning, and she wasn't naïve enough to believe that it was over yet. In all likelihood, it was just starting. She had been waiting for the other shoe to drop all morning. She simply hadn't expected it in the form of this speculative, attractive stranger.

But that was exactly the form it was taking, and she knew it. This speculative, attractive stranger was *him*—the man she'd been wondering about all morning. Now that she knew his name, his face, she almost yearned for her old ignorance. She caught his dark, probing gaze once more and knew that he had been much less disturbing when he had been a stranger.

She felt the fight draining out of her as she opened the envelope. A quit-claim deed and a partnership agreement slid out onto her desk. She stared at them for a long moment, then finally lifted her eyes to Gage's dark, watchful ones.

"So," she said softly, "it was you. Why didn't you tell me right away? On second thought, scratch that question. Giving answers is obviously against your religion."

Another slow grin spread over his face. "That's better," he murmured.

Jenny's heart fluttered oddly at the seemingly unfounded appreciation she saw in his smile. "What's better?" she asked, her voice faintly strangled as he held her in that powerful gaze.

"Your flippancy. It . . . suits you. I was afraid that you wouldn't fight back, and that would be . . . well, boring."

His voice was the seductive but dangerous purr of a jaguar. Jenny felt it stroking her temper into a fine blaze just when she thought she had no strength left to be irritated with. She glared up at him. "I issue fair warning," she answered equally as softly. "I'm getting angry. And my flippancy is nothing compared to my anger. I suggest that you start coming up with some answers, Mr. Pierce. Stop playing games with me. I didn't drive up here to provide you with entertainment for the day."

Once again, a slow, satisfied smile touched his mouth. He got up from the desk and walked back to the sofa, then very nearly managed to pull the rug completely out from under her by chuckling. Jenny stared at him in baffled, helpless frustration.

"I was, wasn't I?" he asked after a moment, the smile still lingering on his lips. "Playing games with you, that is. You know, the God's honest truth is that I didn't mean to. I had no intention of doing that when I walked in here. All I intended to do was talk you into dissolving this partnership and go on my way. But that look on your face just got to me. I didn't think you'd be the type to get rattled so easily, and I guess I started to get a kick out of your reactions."

His smile finally reached his eyes. Without that cold, assessing look, his chiseled face was actually very handsome. Not just attractive, but strikingly sexy. Jenny couldn't help but catch her breath.

Then, gradually, his words penetrated her surprise. As they registered, her control snapped. The weight of the whole morning crashed down on her suddenly, and she jumped to her feet again, her pulse thundering in fury. It was all she could do to keep from shouting at him as she left her desk to face him, her hands clenched at her sides as she tried to control herself.

"I find it hard to believe that you could have any expectations of me. You don't know me," she pointed out hotly. "But just for the record, I *do* get rattled occasionally. Mornings like this, for instance, do the job nicely. Within four hours, Mr. Pierce, I've learned that my father was buried yesterday without anyone waiting until I could get up here for the funeral, or even having the decency to notify me of when it would be. I've learned that some anonymous person has bought into Timber House—an inn that has been owned solely by my family since 1842. Either no one knew or no one was saying who that anonymous person was, and now I find out that it's someone who's walked in here with a chip on his shoulder the size of Mount Rushmore. To top all of this off, the hotel has been neglected so badly by this anonymous partner—you—and my father, that it's about to fall down into a pile of firewood with the next good wind. Business has been horrendous, but, because the land the inn's sitting on is obviously valuable, a group calling themselves International

Hospitality Corporation wants to buy the place anyway. The Oregon Historical Society has caught wind of this and has taken to the driveway with picket signs in order to prevent what was once a mere lumberjack's lodge from being torn down. Oh, and did I forget the ferry? They had representatives waiting for me at the dock just to make sure that I was aware of all this. Unfortunately, at that time, I wasn't aware of *anything*. I thought they were my lawyers and made a total fool out of myself. And you—" She broke off abruptly to take a deep, shaky breath. "You, Mr. Pierce, have the audacity to walk in here and play games with me to see how rattled you can get me. Well, let me give you a clue. You haven't done it yet. But you're close. Your first hint that I'm getting rattled is when I walk over to that bookshelf and start hurling heavy objects at you. When it happens, please clear out. I'm not up for a murder rap today."

She finished suddenly, the adrenaline rushing out of her as rapidly as it had claimed her. For a long moment, they only stared at each other, both of them shocked by her outburst.

Then, infuriatingly, he laughed.

The sound was rich and full, like well-aged wine. It took her a moment to break away from the spell it cast over her, a moment before she shrugged out from beneath the almost irresistible temptation to laugh with him. She took a few threatening steps toward the bookshelf, but he only laughed harder.

"Don't," she warned him, grasping an old ivory figurine. "After the day I've been through, I'd have every right to plead temporary insanity. I'd be out in six months. It's not worth it."

His chuckles died slowly. He attempted to speak several times, then only shook his dark head. Eventually, he pulled himself up from the sofa and went back to her desk.

"You're certainly not cold, are you, Jenny Oliver?" he murmured over the last of his laughter. His voice was suddenly so soft, she doubted if she had heard him correctly.

He looked back at her, his expression sobering somewhat. "Answers," he went on. "As I remember it, you wanted answers." He picked up the quit-claim deed and smoothed it out on her desk. "This, Jenny Oliver, means simply that six months ago, your father turned over all of his interest in Timber House to a partnership we named, for the sake of simplicity, Pierce-Oliver Enterprises. There was only one enterprise, the inn that you've come to inherit, but—"

"Is it safe for me to assume that the house wasn't included?" she interrupted him tersely, but there was an infuriating thread of panic in her voice. "Roughly translated, do I have a place to sleep tonight?"

He gave her a startled look that quickly faded into a slow, unreadable smile that was as disturbing as his watchful eyes had been. "Well, *I* don't own the house," he answered. "I suppose it's yours unless that aunt who buried your father yesterday has laid claim to it. And—" he paused "—if that's the case, you can always stay with me."

His smile didn't reveal any more than his eyes did. Yet there was something steady and provocative about it that made her mouth feel suddenly dry.

Stay with him?

"I'd feel more comfortable on a park bench," she muttered shakily, looking away from him quickly. She knew suddenly and without a doubt that he would understand that she wasn't being sarcastic or flippant this time. She knew because in that split-second that their eyes had met, they had recognized each other. They were, in one respect, at least, kindred spirits. Neither of them was quite what the other had expected. And neither of them was fully prepared to cope with what they had found.

Jenny shook her head nervously and sank down on the sofa. The cushions were still warm from where he had been sitting, and she shifted sideways awkwardly and instinctively.

"She . . . my aunt, that is . . . hasn't—and probably won't—lay claim to anything," she rushed on disjointedly, trying to put their strange moment of communication behind them. "She's an aunt by marriage only and she already has my uncle's share of the original Oliver estate. The house and the inn went to my father. Likewise to me."

Gage stared at her a moment longer, then nodded. "Which brings us to this other piece of paper," he went on. He held up the partnership agreement for her inspection. "This means that of all of that interest which your father turned over to Pierce-

Oliver Enterprises, I own one half and he owns—owned—the other. Unfortunately, this agreement states that in the event of one of the partners' deaths, all interest passes on to his heirs, successors, and assignees, and the partnership remains in full effect. That means us. Any questions?"

Jenny's eyes snapped back to him as he finished. She collected herself and squared her shoulders doggedly as she got to her feet again. "Just one," she answered jauntily. "How much do you want?"

She had the satisfaction of seeing another startled look touch his unreadable eyes. "For my share of Timber House?" he asked. Then his surprise was gone and his raven eyes were shrewd and assessing again. She guessed that he hadn't expected such a question from her so soon or so easily.

"That's right," she responded in her most professional, neutral voice. "You said that you came here to talk me into dissolving the partnership. So let's do it."

He searched her face for a moment before answering. "Okay," he agreed eventually. Then he added, "Three million should do it."

Jenny froze in her tracks as she reached her desk and turned to stare at him. "Three—" she began, then broke off abruptly. She couldn't help herself. She laughed, but there was a thin trace of hysteria in the sound.

"Let me get this straight," she tried again, dropping down into her chair. "You want three million dollars for *half* of Timber House?"

He gave her a level look, then nodded. "That's right. Half of the six million that International Hospitality is offering," he answered pointedly.

"That's six times what you reportedly paid my father!" she exploded.

"*Before* International Hospitality's offer," he reminded her.

"International Hospitality has nothing to do with this. I'm not going to sell to them."

"If you don't, I will."

"Good luck! They're not going to buy half a hotel!"

Their words blasted through the nearly empty office like

gunshots. Long after they had fallen silent, their eyes continued to hold in a defiant battle of wills and the echo of their shouts hung in the air. Jenny glanced away first, embarrassed, then shifted uncomfortably in her chair.

"Let's get one thing straight, Mr. Pierce," she tried to say more softly. "I'll admit that I have no idea what I'm going to do with this place. When I got off the ferry this morning, I had no inkling that this . . . this . . . disaster area was waiting for me. I thought I was coming back to Little Beach for a funeral, and to check in with the managers of an ancient old inn that I'd inherited. I thought that all I'd have to do was give them my phone number and go on my merry way. I've packed only enough for three days. At this point, I don't know if I'm staying or leaving, managing or selling. It's not farfetched to assume that I could move back to Little Beach tomorrow and pick up the reins here myself. I should mention, however, that I don't want to do that. I love San Francisco, I love the hotel I manage there—one a good bit more modern and exciting than this place, I might add—and, to be perfectly honest with you, I want to go home!" She realized almost distantly that her voice was becoming strident. She took a deep breath and tried to bring it down to a more respectable level.

"As far as I'm concerned," she went on, almost whispering now with the effort, "there's only one certainty in my world right now. I might sell my share out to you, I might sell out to John Doe down the street, but I will *not* sell out to International Hospitality. I'm all for dissolving the partnership, but we're going to have to find another way to do it. That International wants the land and not the building is fact, not rumor. I won't see this place torn down. Call it an emotional decision if you like, but I won't change my mind. I grew up here. I played with my teddy bear on the floor where you're standing, and so did my father before me. Therefore, Mr. Pierce, if you want to talk about dissolving partnerships, then just tell me what you'll give me for my share or what you want for for yours—*not* what think you can get from International. International is simply out of the question."

He stared at her enigmatically for a moment before he pushed himself off the desk. Her stomach squirmed as she watched him pace to the center of the room and waited for his response. His face gave her no clue as to what it might be.

"Wait a minute," he drawled after a moment. "Are we talking teddy bears, or are we talking investments?"

Jenny scowled at him. She had no idea what he was getting at. "Pardon me?" she answered warily.

"I'll level with you, Jenny Oliver. I never expected you to be the type to pay homage to teddy bears."

She was on her feet again in an instant. She was shaking, but whether from an exhausted nervous system or rage was hard to tell. Marshaling every last ounce of her dignity, she glared at him.

"I've just spent half an hour of very valuable time trying to help you understand my position," she began tightly, "and all you can do is stand there and speculate about what you expected of me—and not very kindly, I might add. Well, let's get one thing straight, Mr. Pierce. You might be my partner—for the time being—but nowhere is it written in this partnership agreement that I have to put up with this. Please leave. Take a crash course in manners and conducting business meetings, then come back tomorrow." She shoved the agreements back into the envelope and held it out to him in a silent challenge.

Gage returned her gaze with the same thoughtful look that he had been wearing since he had arrived, then finally took the envelope from her and followed her to the door. Jenny grabbed the knob and flung it open with such force that it banged resoundingly against the wall. For a moment, she wondered wildly if the whole inn was going to come tumbling down around them, and she had to bite her lip against more hysterical laughter.

Gage took a single step into the corridor, then stopped. "So much for expectations," he murmured idly, almost as though he were discussing the weather. Jenny looked at him blankly. She'd anticipated anger at her outburst, controlled anger, slow and cold and complete with a reciprocal jab or two of his own. Instead, he only looked down at her with an odd, almost nonexistent smile.

"I thought you'd be ready, eager, and willing to unload this place," he went on. "With Ed gone, I thought you'd be anxious to sever your last tie to the island. I took you to be a big-city girl, not a small-town dreamer, not someone who'd cool her heels here any longer than was necessary. Actually, I'm still not so sure I was wrong. I can't quite figure out why you don't want to accept the offer from International—but it'll come to me. And given enough time, I'll bring you into my camp. You might be the whiz of Warwick Towers, but you're no match for me, Jenny Oliver. I always get what I want . . . especially when it comes to business."

She shouldn't have been surprised that he knew so much about her, not any longer. He had been Ed's friend; Ed had obviously talked about her. Still, hearing him mention the name of the hotel she managed in San Francisco, hearing him speak of the reputation she'd built for herself as manager there, made the same strange vulnerability begin to surface again. His knowledge of her made her feel so exposed, so defenseless—especially since she knew so little about him. She turned wide eyes on him, but he only continued unperturbedly.

"In the meantime, I don't think I want to buy you out. I don't particularly want the inn. I neither want nor need another career challenge, and this place would most definitely be a challenge. No, I want my money back."

It took her a minute to recover enough to realize that he was talking business again. "You were content enough to own half the place while Ed was alive," she blurted out. "Why not own the whole thing now?"

His answering grin was as slow as his voice and a good bit cooler. "Because Ed was my friend. It wasn't a business thing with him. It was more like lending a helping hand."

"But I'm not your friend," she finished for him irritably.

He raised an eyebrow at her. "To tell you the truth, I don't know what you are. But I do know that buying you out—or even maintaining my investment in Timber House with you at the reins—would be too much like going back to work for my taste. I'm retired, and I intend to stay that way. So what I do depends a lot on what you do, I suppose." He paused to give her another shrewd look. "I'd say it's time for you to make a few decisions, Jenny Oliver. It looks to me as though you're going to have to make up your mind whether you're going to stay or go . . . once and for all."

For a moment, she had the uncanny feeling that he was talking about more than the hotel. But that was ridiculous. As though to prove it, he went on matter-of-factly.

"Therefore, it looks to me as though we're going to have to talk again later if we're going to reach an agreement regarding what to do with this albatross." He waved a hand airily to indicate the hotel.

Jenny stared at him for a moment as she tried to get a grip on the conversation again, then bit her lip against the sudden, shocking threat of tears. Albatross, she thought bitterly. She'd come back for a funeral, and she'd ended up with an albatross and a stranger who watched her as though he were the living image of her conscience. She had a crazy urge to pinch herself to see if she were having a nightmare. Then Gage spoke again, his gravelly voice so real and close that she knew she didn't need to. Unfortunately, she wasn't dreaming.

"So you cry, too," he murmured so softly that she had to wonder if she had heard him correctly.

She gave him a desperate look as she blinked back her tears. "Why should that surprise you?" she hissed, feeling at the end of her rope.

He shrugged. "Expectations again, I suppose."

It was the straw that broke the camel's back. Jenny tossed her hair over her shoulder in a gesture of defiance and met his eyes. "Suppose you tell me something new?" she snapped. "Suppose you tell me just what it was that Ed told you about me?" Then she repeated the thought that had been whirling through her mind since he had first arrived. "Suppose you tell me *what* you expect of me?"

He studied her wordlessly for so long that she began to wonder if he would answer her. When he turned on his heel and started down the hall, she was sure he wouldn't. But then he reached the elevator, pushed the Down button, and looked back at her.

"The woman who didn't even know that her father had cancer. That's what I expected," he called back to her in a voice that was as jaded as she had once thought his eyes were. "She's in there somewhere behind those pretty silver eyes. I'd put money on it. You're right—Ed talked about you. A lot. So I know all about you, Jenny Oliver. I'm not a stranger. I'm just praying like hell that I *am* a few other things—like intelligent enough to remember that leopards don't often change their spots, not even when they cry."

Jenny watched, feeling unaccountably stung, as the elevator doors finally groaned open and he disappeared inside. In the second before they closed again, he called out three more words.

"See you around." There was a clanging sound of metal meeting metal as the doors closed. Then he was gone.

Jenny collapsed against the doorjamb as the elevator growled away. "Not if I can help it," she muttered, then stepped back inside and slammed the door.

The problem was, she was beginning to have a sneaking suspicion that she couldn't.

2

Within a week, she knew that she had been right.

Avoiding Gage Pierce was roughly akin to avoiding the steady rain that had been drenching the southern Oregon coast for days. Jenny was quickly becoming resigned to the fact that both would be forces to be reckoned with as long as she remained in Little Beach. To escape either of them would mean leaving the provincial little town. Unfortunately, *that* was something she just couldn't seem to bring herself to do.

Her conscience wouldn't let her. Just as she had told Gage the first day he had stolen into her life, she couldn't bring herself to turn her back on the inn. Every time she closed her eyes, she saw teddy bears.

She scowled at the thought as she walked through the lobby, then made a sudden detour in the direction of the west wall and the double sliding-glass doors there. The doors had been her father's contribution, like the widow's walk had been her great-grandfather's. Not much of the old lumberjack's lodge had remained like it was; it was a potpourri now of various Olivers' tastes. Wings and rooms had been added by the handful over the course of the years. Fur trappers had built the original lodge; lumberjacks had expanded upon it to fit their own needs. Then the Olivers had come along and had bastardized it in their own well-meaning way. Yet the inn was still, even in its present rundown state, authentic enough to have the Oregon Historical Society up in arms over the thought of losing it. Every room had a past; every nook and cranny had a story to tell. Jenny simply couldn't bring herself to abandon it.

She couldn't help believing that she might very well be the inn's last chance. If she failed, if she couldn't set it back on its feet, then she would have no choice but to sell out her share. And if she did that, Gage Pierce would almost certainly end up with full ownership. He hadn't produced five hundred thousand dollars to buy out half of her father's interest in the inn by virtue of good luck. No, he had earned that money, and Jenny suspected that he had done it the hard way. He was a shrewd man. She knew that. She'd seen it time and time again in his eyes. And she knew that no matter whom she sold her share out to, Gage Pierce would find a way to buy it back from them. And he would turn right around and make a fortune by selling it all to International. And *their* first move would be to tear the proud old building down.

So after centuries of owners, it all came down to her. She had to hold on to her share, and she had to make it worth something. What a formidable challenge! she thought. And what a sucker I am for being needed. If only her own father had known her well enough to understand that, he could have brought her back to Little Beach a thousand times. But he hadn't known, and it had taken his death for her to understand that she was needed here. And knowing that, she couldn't leave. No matter how much she longed for the flawless routine and prestige of the hotel she had left behind in San Francisco, she knew that she'd never be able to turn her back on Timber House.

Not yet, anyway. Not until she managed to find a way to buy out Gage Pierce and ensure that the inn stayed in the Oliver family, and not until she had returned it to the fine, rustic establishment it had once been.

"A tall order," she muttered aloud to herself, pushing away

from the glass. She wasn't exactly sure yet how she was going to go about it, but she knew that she'd do it. Gage Pierce might not believe that she was any match for him, but she knew her business. What was more, she couldn't turn away from a challenge, and she couldn't resist being needed.

She threw a final, grim look out the door and turned away. Beyond the rough-hewn deck that extended almost to the edge of the cliff, rain and the sea battered the rocky slope. The sight was somehow soothing. But soothing her taut nerves was something that would have to wait until later. Much later. She still had a whole schedule full of projects to take care of—all of them intended to rescue Timber House before it collapsed or went bankrupt, whichever came first. At the moment, it looked like a toss-up, she thought sourly.

Most of the staff had already assembled in the banquet room by the time she got there. A quick glance at their expectant faces told Jenny that the only people who were missing were the ones who had just come on shift, and she would get to them later. She didn't waste time on preliminaries. She sat down on the edge of one of the tables and dredged up a smile.

Waving a hand to indicate that she was talking about the banquet room, she announced, "Astronomers have nothing on us when it comes to empty space. My friends, you are looking at exactly three thousand square feet of absolutely nothing."

Several pairs of startled eyes glanced around the room. A few people caught her meaning and nodded.

"This room hasn't been used since last August," she went on. "That was ten months ago, and it was also the only time during that year that any kind of function was held here. That translates to one function in eighteen months, for those of you who are still counting." She paused to flash a teasing grin at the accounting department's Horace Tompkins, who had just begun to reach for his ever-present pocket calculator. The standing joke was that his brain had long since been absorbed into the gadget.

"I've got a suggestion," someone piped up from the back of the room. "We could always move cots in here for the staff. We already spend more time at these meetings than we do at home."

Jenny couldn't help but laugh along with everyone else. The truth of the matter was that they had had a meeting every day that week on one subject or another. To the staff's credit, no one was really complaining. Most of them had worked at Timber House for as long as Jenny could remember and were as concerned with saving it as she was. She also suspected that they appreciated being included in her efforts to restore it. Though no one had said as much, Jenny guessed that her father had neither taken their suggestions into consideration nor solicited their help. He would have been too hard-headed, too proud. Yet Jenny knew that these people probably saw more areas for potential improvement than she did. They were the ones who were closest to every daily facet of the operation.

Knowing that, she also knew that she needed their support. She didn't mind waiting for the laughter to die down. It was all in the interest of morale. She kept a smile on her own lips as she reached for her notes, then finally cleared her throat as a signal that she wanted to get on with the meeting.

Then her smile froze.

The double doors leading out onto the lobby swung open and Gage strode into the room. A few people twisted in their seats to see who had come in, but basically no one interpreted his presence as an interruption. No one but Jenny. She watched him through narrowed eyes as he silently made his way across the back of the room and stepped behind the bar.

He was doing it again.

Her nerves stretched until they felt like thin, taut wires and her knuckles whitened as she clutched her notes. She knew his routine by heart now. She felt as though she had been coping with it for a year instead of a mere week. She silently predicted each of his next movements as he poured himself a Scotch and water, took a thoughtful sip, lit a cigarette, then hoisted himself up to sit at the edge of the bar.

His eyes never left her.

She knew that it was all just part of the strange game he had been playing with her all week, but that didn't prevent two bright spots of color from appearing on her cheeks. His individual actions varied occasionally—sometimes he simply appeared in doorways or had some legitimate business to attend to—but the bottom line was that those burning black eyes had been following her everywhere since the moment she had first set foot back in Timber House. Sometimes his appearances seemed orchestrated to elicit the most reaction from her—like now. Yet at other times, she was sure that he didn't even realize what he was doing. His look was challenging and mocking at the moment, but she had known it to be so distant and speculative that sometimes she even had to wonder if he was really seeing her.

And she had no idea why he was doing it.

She'd tried talking to him. She'd tried again and again to find out just what it was about her that required such great thought. His obsidian eyes were always waiting, too often brooding, and too rarely lit with a smile. He made her feel as though she were some strange specimen beneath glass that wasn't behaving quite the way the encyclopedia said she should. And that frustrated her more than she'd ever dreamed possible. She was a woman who was used to speculation; she'd worked her way up in the ranks at Warwick Towers much too rapidly to be able to avoid raised eyebrows. Yet the thick skin she'd developed didn't seem to offer her any protection against Gage Pierce. His constant perusal unbalanced her time and time again. It left her feeling jittery and nervous . . . and too often flushed with a strange heat that was as obvious as it was uncomfortable.

She shook her head absently as though to convince herself that he wasn't really watching her again, then turned her full attention back to the staff, most of whom were looking at her curiously now. Or, more accurately, she thought, she *tried* to give them her full attention. Gage's eyes kept boring into her with smoldering intent until her nerves felt scorched and battered and composure became a struggle.

She cleared her throat yet again. "I, uh, I've compiled a little bit of information here through some judicious sniffing." Out of the corner of her eye, she saw Gage take another mouthful of his drink. She didn't have to look directly at him to know that he hadn't glanced away from her while he'd done it.

"There are, uh, two major hotels in Longport City," she forced herself to go on. "Both of them offer much more modern facilities than we can boast of, but neither do they have the charm and atmosphere of Timber House."

"Charm? Where?"

This time the laughter was subdued. Everyone knew that charm was one thing Timber House had been severely lacking lately. There was little of it to be found in patched sofa cushions.

Jenny squared her shoulders doggedly at the thought and pushed on. "That's just it," she argued. "The charm's here; it's just buried under years of neglect. Because of that, the people of Little Beach have been taking their business to the hotels in Longport City. And this is no small transference of loyalty we're talking about here. When Mr. and Mrs. McDaniel chose to hold their daughter's wedding reception over there, they had to foot the bill to get three hundred people across the bay on the ferry. Obviously, they would have preferred to have held the function at Timber House—if Timber House had had anything to offer them."

He was still doing it, still staring at her. Though Jenny struggled to keep her mind on the issue at hand, the enthusiasm in her voice began to drag. By the time she finished, her tone sounded strained. She shot him a searing look over the heads of the people who were beginning to look at her oddly.

A shadow of a smile touched his lips and he raised his glass at her in a silent toast. She nearly choked as her heart formed a sudden, fluttering lump in her throat. What was he doing to her? And *why?*

"Therefore," someone spoke up, his voice sounding incredibly distant as Jenny's eyes locked with Gage's, "we've got to come up with something to offer them."

She pulled her eyes back to the crowd to search for the man who had spoken. "Precisely," she agreed quickly, then immediately shook her head. "Uh, what I meant was, rather, the point I was trying to make was—we *have* something to offer. We've just got to dig it out from beneath the debris and polish it up. This place has *history,* it's got soul. It's got more to offer than both those hotels in Longport City put together. People ought to be ferrying over here to come to us instead of the other way around."

"Spoken like a true Little Beach native," Gage drawled. She glanced up at him to see that same slight smile. No one else seemed to recognize the taunt in his words, but it sounded crystal-clear to her. She glared at him furiously.

"We've got a lot to work with. The basics are here," she went on tightly, trying to ignore him. "I mean, just look at this one room. The fireplace is *original,* for God's sake. It's been here since the place was built in 1798. This room was the original lodge. Everything else was built off of it. If that's not the stuff charm is made of, I don't know what is. Take the bar, for instance. It—"

She broke off suddenly as she pointed in that direction, remembering too late that Gage was still perched on it. As soon as she pointed to him, the subtle mockery in his smile disappeared. All the staff saw was a warm grin and an acknowledgment in the form of a nod of his head. Jenny's train of thought became completely derailed.

"What about the bar?" someone asked. Although the older employees had been with Timber House long enough to know every angle of its history, this was all news to most of the younger ones. Jenny's gaze swiveled from the man who had asked the question to Gage and then back again as she tried to remember what she had been about to say.

Her mind was blank.

Gage hopped down from the bar and moved behind it to fix himself another drink. The easy grace of his walk emphasized his studied casualness. She noticed that he had rolled up his shirt sleeves and that his forearms were dark with silky black hairs. Whatever she had been about to say regarding the bar was so far removed from her brain as she watched him that she knew she'd never remember it.

Horace Tompkins reached out and tapped her calf gently with the end of his pen. Jenny jumped slightly, wrenching her eyes back to the slight, bespectacled man. "You were telling us about

First Class Romance

Delivered to your door by

Silhouette Desire®

(See inside for special 4 FREE book offer)

Find romance at your door with 4 FREE Silhouette Desire novels!

Now you can have the intense romances you crave without searching for them. You can receive Silhouette Desire novels each month to read in your own home. Silhouette Desire novels are modern love stories for readers who want to experience firsthand *all* the joyous and thrilling emotions of women who fall in love with a passion that knows no bound. You can share in the passion and joy of their love, every month, when you subscribe to Silhouette Desire.

By filling out and mailing the attached postage-paid order card, you'll receive FREE 4 new Silhouette Desire romances (a $9.00 value) plus a FREE Mystery Gift. You'll also receive an extra bonus: our monthly Silhouette Books Newsletter.

Approximately every 4 weeks, we'll send you 6 more Silhouette Desire novels to examine FREE for 15 days. If you decide to keep them, you'll pay just $11.70 (a $13.50 value) with no charge for home delivery and at no risk! You'll also have the option of cancelling at any time. Just drop us a note. Your first 4 books and the Mystery Gift are yours to keep in any case.

Silhouette Desire®

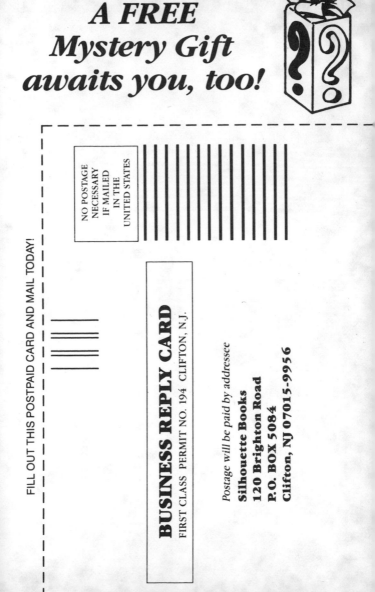

A FREE
Mystery Gift
awaits you, too!

Mail this card today for your
4 FREE BOOKS
(a $9.00 value) and a Mystery Gift FREE!

Silhouette **Desire**®

Silhouette Books, 120 Brighton Rd., P.O. Box 5084, Clifton, NJ 07015-9956

☐ Yes, please send 4 new Silhouette Desire novels and a Mystery Gift to my home FREE and without obligation. Unless you hear from me after I receive my 4 FREE books, please send me 6 new Silhouette Desire novels for a free 15-day examination each month as soon as they are published. I understand that you will bill me a total of just $11.70 (a $13.50 value) with no additional charges of any kind. There is no minimum number of books that I must buy, and I can cancel at any time. No matter what I decide, the first 4 books and the Mystery Gift are mine to keep.

NAME _____
(please print)

ADDRESS _____

CITY _____ STATE _____ ZIP _____

Terms and prices subject to change.
Your enrollment is subject to acceptance by Silhouette Books.

CAD325

the potential this room has," he reminded her in a half whisper that was entirely too loud for her comfort.

It took everything she had to nod at him and then concentrate on the meeting again. "Right," she answered more harshly than was necessary. "Why don't we all meet this time tomorrow night and pool our suggestions? There's got to be a way to utilize what we've got here—you know, to play it up, yet still make drastic improvements." As she spoke, Gage finished fixing his drink, lit another cigarette, and moved around to a barstool. "Uh, six o'clock tomorrow night," she finished hastily.

She was too preoccupied to notice the perplexed frowns the staff exchanged as they filed out of the room. She kept her eyes carefully on her notes, realizing too late that all the points she had planned to make had been in front of her the whole time, but she had been too frazzled to remember that. Too frazzled and too rattled by Gage Pierce. The thought ignited her. As the last person shuffled out of the room, she launched herself to her feet in fury.

He lifted an eyebrow at her as she approached him. "You look like Joan of Arc preparing for battle," he commented.

"Ah, but it's you who's going to burn at the stake," she answered heatedly, slapping her notes down on the bar.

"Don't I get some kind of trial first? I don't even know what I'm guilty of."

"You're—" She broke off abruptly, realizing the paranoia of what she had been about to say: You're driving me out of my mind the way you've been staring at me? I'm going to go crazy if you keep popping up out of the blue to lurk in the shadows where no one but I can see you? No way, she thought grimly. He'd waste maybe thirty seconds before he'd call the nearest funny farm and have her committed. If she was going to fight him for full control of Timber House, she was going to have to do it without the encumbrance of a straitjacket.

She marshalled her thoughts quickly and attacked him on the basis of the next logical thing that came to her mind. "It was incredibly rude of you to interrupt this meeting that way," she snapped.

He looked too innocent. His eyes widened until she was sure that he was mocking her. "Rude?" he repeated.

"Yes, rude, damn it! You broke up the meeting! How am I ever supposed to get this place back on its feet if you keep foiling me at every turn?"

His eyes held hers over the rim of his glass as he took another sip. "I realize that you hate to be reminded of this," he answered eventually, "but I am your partner. I haven't committed any breach of etiquette. I own the place. I have every right to sit in on staff meetings. Speaking of which, that is precisely what I did. I sat in on a meeting. I fail to see how you can misconstrue that to mean I was foiling your efforts, which, I might add, seem a bit overzealous to me. You've had these people here every night this week. Are you trying to build Rome in a day?"

Jenny glowered at him. "I'd try to do it in an hour if I thought it was possible. Anything to raise enough money to get you out of the picture and the International wolves away from the door."

Gage lifted his eyebrows at her sarcastically. "In that order?"

Her eyes narrowed as she searched his face, trying to figure out what he was getting at. "They're not mutually exclusive goals," she responded at length. "If you were out of the picture, International wouldn't be a threat. *I'm* certainly not planning to sell to them."

He appraised her silently for a moment. "You know, you present a hell of a good argument when you're not being hot-headed. Sort of like the prodigal daughter I expected you to be. You ought to be more careful, Jenny Oliver. Every once in a blue moon, your mask slips. Just a bit, but enough to remind me that behind those silver eyes, a leopard is trying to get out, spots intact."

For a moment, she could only stare at him, all of her impulses churning in confusion. Then she remembered his parting words on the day that he had first stalked his way into her life. *Leopards don't often change their spots, even when they cry.* She hadn't really understood then, except to the extent that he seemed to be saying he thought he knew all of her vices and shortcomings. She didn't really understand any more than that now. But she *did* know that she wasn't going to tolerate his inane suppositions any longer.

She tossed her hair over her shoulder defiantly and jumped into the argument feet first. "Is that what you've been waiting for?" she demanded bluntly. "For my so-called mask to slip so that you can determine that all of my nasty little spots are exactly what you thought they were? For me to turn out to be the person you've got all these strange expectations of?"

His gaze was level, his smile chiding. He lifted an eyebrow at her provokingly. "Well, all things come around to he who will but wait," he drawled after a moment.

"Then pack yourself a lunch, because you're going to have a long wait," she snapped before she could bite her tongue. "What you see is what you get."

His eyes lit immediately and his grin became wide. The chuckle that escaped him was deep and throaty. She understood suddenly that he'd been playing with her again.

And she'd taken the bait.

Anger burned through her, both at her own gullibility and at him. Yet before she could open her mouth a second time, his eyes were remote again, his voice so distant that she almost couldn't hear it.

"That's the problem with good eyesight. You see too many inconsistencies," he murmured.

Just a handful of words, and he'd robbed her of any kind of retort. Jenny frowned at him in confusion. "I'd settle for good hearing," she muttered, disgruntled. "What earthshaking point are you trying to make now . . ."

She trailed off as his watchful eyes snagged hers again, cutting her off more effectively than if he had actually interrupted her. Those eyes had been her undoing for a week. They were a shaman's eyes, she thought wildly. Deep, dark, and disturbing. And powerful. Too powerful. Like the man himself.

"No matter," he finished, obviously mistaking her silence as a form of surrender. "At the moment, I've got a more important point to make. You might want to build Rome in a day, but I think you ought to take the feelings of the staff into consideration.

Business might be your life's blood, but I'd wager that at least half of those women here tonight have hungry families waiting at home for them. Do you realize that it's six-thirty? They went off shift over an hour ago. They should be home feeding their kids by now."

Jenny grappled with the conversation a moment, realized that he was talking about the inn again, then gave him an odd look. "You know, I can't figure out if you're just playing champion of the people to antagonize me, or if you're an honest-to-God, died-in-the-wool chauvinist."

"Both, probably." Suddenly, he was grinning again, one of his rare, genuine grins. "You antagonize so well," he said.

It wasn't what she needed to hear. More than ever before, she wanted to grab him by the shoulders and demand to know why he should want to antagonize her in the first place. But she knew. He'd told her. She just didn't want to remember or admit it to herself. He enjoyed her reactions, and she gave them to him by the handful with the least provocation.

Instead of giving him the satisfaction of another one, she moved around behind the bar and poured herself a hefty snifter of brandy. She was sure he'd only give her another of the smug, cryptic responses he was so adept at if she pushed the subject . . . and she was so clumsy at rebounding those smug, cryptic responses.

She swallowed some of the brandy and took a deep breath. "Mr. Pierce," she began slowly, carefully, but then he cut her off.

"Call me Gage. We see so much of each other, it's silly to cling to proprieties."

This time she knew that he was goading her. She didn't even reward him with a dark look. She smiled at him as sweetly as she could manage and purred, "Fine. Gage, then. You don't 'own the place,' Gage. You own *half* of it. I own the other half. That means we're really going to have to learn to sidestep each other better if you're going to continue to refuse to sell your share to me. Something tells me that this is *not* the way to go about it."

Gage shrugged. "I haven't decided *what* I'm going to do with my share yet." He grinned at her again somewhat crookedly. His expression was definitely that of a man who was enjoying himself.

"If you remember, I was waiting for you to make a decision about what you're going to do with yours."

"I've made one," she replied impulsively. "I'm keeping it. I'm staying."

She had the satisfaction of seeing him look genuinely surprised. Obviously, it was the last thing in the world he expected her to say. "For how long?" he asked.

"For as long as it takes me to buy you out at a reasonable price," she answered grimly.

"A reasonable price? I suppose that means anything other than International's price?" His eyes became brighter with genuine interest.

"Precisely." She spoke the word succinctly as she held his gaze. Nothing about her revealed that she was shaking inside, wondering just what she had gotten herself into. One didn't argue with a man with a shaman's eyes. But, then, she'd never really been one to heel to common sense. She was one to give in to heartfelt passions and causes. And, now that fate had lured her back, Timber House was rapidly becoming both.

"You could have a long wait," Gage pointed out eventually. Jenny scrambled to remember what they had been fencing about this time.

"So I'll pack a lunch," she replied sweetly, remembering. "As a wise man—or perhaps just a very optimistic one—once told me, all things come around to he who will but wait."

Suddenly, he was grinning again, a dazzling white smile that threatened to take her breath away. His eyes were almost the color of a twilight sky now, a deep indigo blue alive with pleasure. As always, just when she'd thought she'd won a battle, he managed to scramble out of the melee with some sort of victory . . . even if it was only to surprise her and render her speechless. She stared at him, struggling for a response as he chuckled.

"You fight dirty, Jenny Oliver," he drawled.

"Sometimes," she managed, unable to pull her eyes away from his, "it's the only way to win."

"And do you always win?" he asked slowly, curiously.

She took a deep, shaky breath, forcing herself to look away

from him. "Only when I want something very badly. As that same man once told me, I always get what I want. And I want Timber House to remain intact."

Silence filled the rambling, empty room as he watched her steadily, obviously weighing her words. Jenny stared stubbornly at the fireplace, afraid to look at him again.

"My words seem to have developed a tendency to haunt me," he murmured after a moment. "I think I'm going to have to watch what I say around you."

"Probably." She turned her attention to her fingernails, still refusing to look up and be caught in that gaze again.

"And vice versa."

She couldn't help herself. Confusion drew her eyes back to his like a magnet. "What?" she breathed. "I don't understand."

His grin was slight and teasing again. "You might want to watch what you say to me," he pointed out too equably. "It might be in your best interest to be nice to me until I decide just what I'm going to do with my half of Timber House."

It never even occurred to her that there was any kind of innuendo in his suggestion. Not from this man. Jenny stared at him blankly, more aware of that subtle grin, which managed to have so many meanings, than she was of his words.

She bristled, but struggled to maintain her composure. "Well, in the meantime," she said, "is this going to continue until you do decide?"

She was rewarded with another flash of surprise in those unreadable eyes. "Is what going to continue?" he asked guardedly.

"Your little routine of lurking in the shadows like some kind of demented ghost until you get me rattled."

His laugh was rich and full as the first time she had heard it. And, like before, it tempted her to laugh, too . . . even if the joke was on her. She bit her lip and glared at him, wondering what was so funny.

"If anyone gets you rattled, Jenny Oliver, it's you. Maybe you ought to work on not letting it happen so easily."

"Like not at all?" she snapped, rallying and forgetting about his laugh. "I think I do a remarkably good job of keeping my cool when you consider what I'm up against."

"A demented ghost?"

"Precisely."

"I can assure you that I'm not a ghost. I'm very much alive."

If you are, I don't want to know about it. The thought jumped into her brain suddenly, startling her. But the idea behind it was clear, too clear for her own comfort. As long as she knew that there was nothing but ice water flowing through his veins, she wasn't attracted to him. As long as he kept brooding, he was only disturbing. But once he became human, once he laughed and smiled and became a man, then he would also become dangerous. He would make it too easy to be drawn to those compelling midnight eyes and that knee-weakening physique.

And she didn't want to be drawn in. She had spent a lifetime learning that to care about people was to be hurt. Ed had taught her well; so had others. She'd learned to surround herself with balanced budgets and inventories. They could be controlled; people could not. Men like Gage Pierce couldn't even come close.

She swallowed hard, forcing herself to respond calmly. "Well, if you're not a ghost, then please stop acting like one," she finally managed to say. "In other words, stop haunting me. If you don't like me, that's fine. Trust me when I tell you that I won't kill myself over it. I would, however, like you to behave rationally. The common practice of a person who doesn't like someone else is to stay away from that person. You might try it."

"When did I ever say that I didn't like you?" His response was quick and oddly attentive.

Jenny responded tightly, "You didn't have to say it. Your talk about my 'spots' has said it all. I don't suppose that if I showed them to you, you'd stop looking for them?"

She regretted her words a second too late to stop them. Gage's smile was different this time, slow and . . . almost seductive. A man's smile. Her breath caught.

"We could try it and see."

"I . . . you—" She broke off and grabbed her notes from the

bar, turning away. She felt flushed and hot again. "When it snows in July," she muttered, recovering slightly and glancing back at him. "In the meantime, just stop lurking in corners, hmm?"

The beginnings of another smile teased his lips. Either he was going to laugh at her again, or he was trying to rattle her. Based on her experience with him, Jenny had to believe that the latter was the case. She stiffened, inwardly steeling herself for his jab, but he only drained his glass and set it down on the bar with a sharp tap.

"I'd love to oblige, but there's one small problem," he answered.

Jenny was too exasperated to hide the groan that rose to her lips. "You own half the place," she supplied sarcastically, mimicking his slow, rusty voice.

"Yep. And as long as I do, I like to keep on top of my investment. I'm just checking up on you, Jenny Oliver. I'm not lurking."

She drew in her breath at his audacity and the affront of having someone check up on her after all these years—especially someone who was an unwanted partner and not the full owner of the hotel she was managing. But while she struggled for a retort, Gage glanced down at his watch, dismissing her rage.

"In the meantime," he went on, "you seem to be doing just fine, so I'll be on my way. I'd stay and chat, but I have an appointment to keep. Keep up the good work, Jenny Oliver. You're on the right track, although you might want to consider charity."

"Charity?" Her voice was only a notch above a whisper as she clutched her notes to her chest protectively and watched him with a befuddled frown. She didn't even know if he was talking about her or the hotel. She didn't know *what* he was talking about.

"Charity. To promote the banquet room," he answered. "The historical society's on your side, isn't it? Let them hold an affair here for free—after you've fixed the room up, of course. Advertise that charm you were talking about. It'll be cheaper than billboards."

Charity. The single word lodged in her throat so tightly that she couldn't even speak it aloud. He was right. It was a brilliant idea.

And she hadn't thought of it.

With a parting smile that she couldn't read—although she could have sworn that it smacked with the triumph of a challenge well met—he turned for the door. She was inches away from sacrificing her self-respect and hurling her glass at him when he paused and turned around.

"Oh, you might want to knock off these after-shift staff meetings, too. As I mentioned, I'm sure those employees have families to get home to."

"You conduct staff meetings your way, and I'll conduct them mine," she answered tightly, straining for control.

His response was almost too outrageous to be believed. "Not while you're my partner, you won't."

She picked up her glass and threw it at him. Long after silence replaced the sound of shattering glass in the banquet room, his rare laughter echoed in her heart, telling her what she was already coming to suspect.

She'd met her match.

3

A week later, Gage suddenly decided that he needed an office. No matter that he had distinctly told her that he didn't want to maintain his investment in Timber House, or that he was retired and intended to stay that way. No matter that he had already survived six months of silent partnership without one. He needed one now.

He laid claim to the cramped room behind the registration desk in the lobby, sharing the limited space there with Horace Tompkins, the other accountant, and a coffee maker that had seen better days. Yet for all of his protests that he now needed desk space, Gage spent very little time vying with Horace and Bud Pullman for it. More often than not, he merely stood behind the registration desk, one broad shoulder braced against the door of the accounting room while—to Jenny's disgruntled way of thinking—he observed his kingdom. Or her. Usually her. Just as he was doing now.

She slanted him a dark look and tried to step around him so that she could get into the accounting room to see Horace. She quickly realized that it was a futile effort, absolutely impossible without brushing up against him. And *that* was something that she definitely didn't care to do. The thought had crossed her mind many times that the best·way to shoulder the burden of Gage's brooding, watchful gaze was to pretend that his powerful masculinity didn't exist. Taken together, they unbalanced her more than she cared to admit. For the sake of her sanity, she didn't want to touch him, not even inadvertently. She didn't want to be reminded of the fact that he was a man. It was much more comforting to think of him as a business problem that needed to be remedied.

When it was at all possible, at any rate. Now was not one of those times. He made no effort to get out of her way as she tried to step past him, but only glanced down at her with a long, considering expression that seemed to make his eyes smolder. His broad shoulders filled the doorframe. His air of self-confidence was shakingly masculine; his smile, when it finally came, was almost devilish. And the opened collar of his shirt revealed matted, curly black hair.

He did not look like a business problem.

Jenny took a quick, involuntary step backward, then glanced up at him with a look of annoyance that was specifically designed to mask the sudden, fluttering panic in the pit of her stomach. "If you're not going to do anything constructive, then the very least you can do is get out of my way," she muttered with forced sarcasm. "Will you please move so that I can get by?"

She was getting to the point where she could recognize that satisfied smile of his from a mile off—he'd been using it that often lately. Unfortunately, it generally meant that she'd reacted just as he'd expected—or hoped—she would. It touched his lips now as he made a great show of stepping into the office. With a dramatic and gallingly cheerful sweep of his arm, he indicated that she should enter.

Jenny scowled and strode past him, making her way to Horace's desk. She shot Gage another brief, dark look, then pointedly turned her attention to the accountant.

"It's a good budget, Horace," she told the man, dropping a file folder in front of him. "There are a few points that I want to go over with you, but I think they can wait until tomorrow. We can

43

discuss them over coffee in the morning if you can make the time. Right now, I think I'm going to call it a day." She gave the man a weak smile as she tried to pretend that Gage's simmering dark eyes weren't taking in her every movement. As always when he was around, her composure was beginning to unravel.

She swallowed hard and left the room, trying to ignore Gage. It didn't work. The sound of his footsteps on the hardwood floor hammered in perfect time with her heart as he sauntered after her. Even before she gave in and turned around, she knew that he had stopped behind the registration desk. He leaned one hip against it and slid his hands into the pockets of his slacks as she watched.

"Going home?" he asked.

"Well . . . no," she answered cautiously. "I thought I'd take a shower and change here." One of the assets of having an office on the fifth floor was that most of the rooms came equipped with small private bathrooms, but he knew that. And considering his preoccupation with offices lately, she decided that it was best not to remind him of the advantages of hers too blatantly. She was liable to find her desk sitting out in the hall the next time she went upstairs, with Gage firmly ensconced in Ed's old quarters.

But Gage let the mention of offices pass by. He looked her over intently, then made a great show of glancing down at his watch. "Eleven hours isn't enough working time for you?" he asked idly. "You've been here since seven thirty this morning, haven't you?"

Jenny felt her hands clench in exasperation. Even after two weeks, she still wasn't able to read him. Comments that seemed suspiciously leading were becoming the norm with him. The worst part was that they usually *were* leading . . . and she always understood their destination too late.

"I'm not planning to work tonight," she answered carefully. "You just heard me telling Horace that I was calling it a day. I'd repeat it all to you personally, but you're going to have to settle for eavesdropping this time. I've got to run. I have a date."

"A date?" His eyes narrowed a bit, becoming even more speculative than before.

"Don't tell me," she drawled sarcastically, surprising even

herself with the sharp, defensive edge that suddenly appeared in her voice. "That must be a spot, too."

"A spot?" he repeated. Now he looked genuinely confused. If he hadn't started a small fire burning inside her by acting so surprised that she had a date, she might have found some satisfaction in the fact that she'd disconcerted him.

"As in leopards," she supplied tersely.

"Oh, that." Now he sounded oddly bored.

"It was your analogy, not mine."

He lifted an eyebrow at her. "Who put the bee in your bonnet today?"

"You did," she retorted irritably. "You always do. You know, you've got an outstanding talent for doing that."

Suddenly, he chuckled. Warm brandy and cigarettes, she thought crazily. When he chuckled, he brought to mind fireplaces and dark hours of the night, a voice satiated with brandy and cigarettes.

"Not so, Jenny Oliver," he murmured at length. "You've just got an outstanding propensity for getting rattled, much as it continually surprises me."

She felt her temper unraveling. It was silly, and she felt like nothing so much as a ten-year-old kid working up to a tantrum, but he was able to do that to her. "Like my date surprises you?" she demanded, disgusted with the sullen echo in her voice but unable to stop it.

He was quiet for so long that she began to doubt that he had heard her . . . and hope that maybe she hadn't said such an asinine thing after all. But then his midnight eyes zeroed in on her again and she knew that he was only digesting what she had said.

True to form, his slow grin capped off his silence. "You're very astute, Jenny Oliver. You're right. Your date surprises me," he admitted.

She scowled at him peevishly. "Why? Women have dates. I'm a woman. Ergo, I'm capable of having dates."

"Somewhere along the line I got the impression that you were much happier with a calculator than with a man."

He'd done it again. A few words, and her retort was lost. She felt the wind billowing out of her sails and her face flushing as she stared at him. After a moment, she gave a tiny sigh of surrender and began to turn away. "You're a brilliant man, Mr. Pierce," she muttered wearily. "Maybe you should have been a psychiatrist."

He shrugged. "Not enough money in it. Why?"

"Why should you have been a psychiatrist?"

"No. Why do you prefer calculators to men?"

He wasn't going to allow her to get off without answering. She had to force herself to shrug casually. A strange feeling of being on the brink claimed her. She knew that the conversation was turning toward dangerous ground. Anything that drew them closer together—confidences, inadvertent touches, honesty—all of it scared her. The only safe thing about the hard, seductive, and disturbing presence of Gage Pierce was his distance. Confidences were one aspect among the many things that could bridge the comfort of that gap.

And yet she heard herself answering anyway. "Not men, necessarily. People," she replied, struggling for flippancy. "Calculators can be controlled. People can't. I like to be in control. Less chance of coming up with the short straw that way, you know?"

A strange play of emotions touched his chiseled features. Jenny scarcely blinked as she watched, afraid that she would miss something. He looked surprised, distrustful, confused . . . all at once. And then he turned away from her abruptly.

"Not the spot you expected?" Jenny heard herself taunting him. "That's the trouble with masks," she pushed. "Sometimes they don't hide anything."

He shot her a warning look as he reached into the accounting office to grab his sport jacket off a coatrack there. "Sometimes, Jenny Oliver," he murmured darkly, "you're just too damned smart for your own good. Go take your shower and get ready for your date. I've got an appointment to keep."

"That doesn't surprise me." God, what was she doing? Why couldn't she just quit while she was ahead? Yet the words kept tumbling out of her. "You have more appointments than the beach has sand," she heard herself continuing. "Just what do you do at these appointments? Buy and sell empires, or just try to deliver small, rundown inns into conglomerate hands?"

"None of the above. I'm retired, remember? Not to mention the fact that I have an uncooperative partner." His dry humor was considerably forced, but she didn't take the hint.

"So what *do* you do in the dark hours after you run out of here?" she persisted. And why did she care? a little voice in the back of her brain nagged.

Gage stopped just as he rounded the registration desk. The look he gave her probably would have sent a less obtuse woman running for cover, she thought sourly, suddenly doubting her intelligence.

"*I* have other interests besides Timber House," he responded slowly.

It was a theme that had been recurring more and more in their clashes lately—his insinuations that the hotel and her responsibility to it were her life. She didn't understand it, but then, she didn't understand a lot of his enigmatic comments.

"So do I," she answered quietly, feeling the fight draining out of her abruptly. Somewhere along the line, provoking him had ceased to be fun. "And one of them starts in about an hour. If you'll excuse me, I've got to get ready for my date," she finished. It occurred to her suddenly that she was making a little too much out of a dinner engagement that meant virtually nothing; if her heart had still been involved, she wouldn't have been going. Yet her throat closed at the thought of telling Gage Pierce that. Was it because she wanted him to think that at least one man found her to be more than a toy to rattle, or because she did, indeed, have other interests besides Timber House? She decided that she didn't want to think about it.

Gage, however, didn't leave her much choice. "Your first love?" he asked abruptly, his voice stopping her as she turned away from the desk. It was laced with strong sarcasm, but something else, too, something demanding and oddly brittle.

"My first crush, more accurately," she answered, watching his eyes warily as she paused. Then she let out a deep breath. "You want to know about Colby Barrett? Okay, I'll tell you about him.

Twelve years ago, he was tall and handsome with these soft brown eyes that could turn your knees to water. Every girl in our class had a crush on him. I was lucky enough—or so I thought at the time—to date him for a year or so. I thought I was in love. But then, I was only seventeen. What did I know about love? He knew more than I did. He knew better than to base a seventeen-year-old life on it, so he went off to college that September. Only he forgot to say good-bye. I never heard from him again until this morning." She chuckled shortly. "He wants to see me again. Tonight. I thought it might be an interesting alternative to the same boring TV shows. Who knows? Maybe he got fat and bald."

Gage was quiet for a long time after she finished. Then he growled, "The sweet taste of revenge, is that it?"

Jenny's eyes widened slightly as she watched him dig his keys out of his pocket with a tight, irate gesture. Had he picked up on the slight edge of bitterness in her voice that she had tried so hard to conceal? Did he somehow know that Colby Barrett was more than just a childhood sweetheart, that he had provided her with her first real taste of rejection from someone other than her father? She'd suspected for the longest while that nothing escaped Gage's shrewd gaze. But were his ears that sharp, too? The thought brought a light shiver to her skin.

"Revenge?" she echoed carefully.

"You sound like you're out to get even with him. Are you planning to waltz up to him tonight looking all polished, beautiful, and successful to prove to him what a great prize he gave up?" he went on, his voice tightening even more. He was obviously warming to the subject.

For a long moment, she could only stare at him as foolish hurt clawed at her stomach. He was being so cold, so hard . . . as though something she had said had angered him. But what? What could he possibly care about Colby Barrett?

"Maybe," she answered finally, defiantly. "Sure. Maybe I *am* out to get even. So what? What's with you? What's so abnormal or villainous about that? Can you honestly stand there and tell me that you wouldn't look forward to seeing your first love again, especially if she walked out on you without a word?"

His eyes narrowed suddenly with some distant thought or memory. For the first time in a long while, she realized how little she really knew about him.

"Only to choke her," he answered coldly. Then he shrugged into his jacket. For a brief moment, she thought she saw that jaded weariness in his eyes again. Then he started toward the door and she couldn't be sure.

Frustration washed over her as she watched him go. "Well, not all of us share your warm, friendly personality! I'll be content just to have dinner with mine!" she shouted after him hotly, finally losing her temper. Would she ever understand anything this man said? Would she ever figure out why it bothered her that she didn't?

He paused long enough to call back to her, "Then by all means, go for it, Jenny Oliver! Enjoy!"

She didn't have to be able to see his eyes to know that his response wasn't quite sincere. She stared after him for a moment, seething, then turned on her heel. She was still shaking when she reached her office and slammed the door behind her.

"I don't know what your problem is, Pierce," she muttered, moving to the window to watch him through narrow eyes as he made his way across the parking lot. "But I'll be damned if I'm going to let it get to me."

Unfortunately, it seemed that she did little else these days. Scowling, she turned away from the window to pour herself a calming glass of brandy.

As she carried it into the bathroom, it occurred to her distantly that she was much more unnerved by Gage Pierce than she was upset by the thought of seeing Colby again. Colby . . . who'd professed to love her, then had left her. He'd dropped her as casually from his life as her father had. She wasn't even very curious about seeing him again.

She was much more curious about the woman Gage Pierce preferred to choke.

4

⁓∘⊚⊚⊛⊚⊛⊛⊚⊛⊛⊚∘⁓

So she had a date. So what? As she had pointed out with that defiant little edge of flippancy, she was a woman, and women had dates. He should hardly be surprised.

But he was surprised. And . . . annoyed. She'd done it to him again. She'd changed. Every time he thought he had her pegged, she'd change. And pegging her had been no easy chore.

No easy chore? He swore deprecatingly. Hell, if he were going to be honest with himself, he'd have to admit that he hadn't really pegged her at all. He still didn't know who she was. Ed's cold, selfish daughter . . . or a spot of indomitable sunlight against the drab, grim backdrop of Timber House? Street-smart lady hotel tycoon . . . or a vulnerable woman who became shaken up at the thought of not having a place to spend the night when she owned half a hotel? He didn't know, couldn't tell. The only thing that he'd become relatively sure of was that she possessed one hell of a suit of armor against men. The proof of it was there in the way she looked at him sometimes, so still and wary and ready to launch into flight if he moved so much as a muscle. It was in the way he was able to rattle her so easily. She didn't trust men. Liked them, sure . . . but she didn't trust them.

Or at least he hadn't thought so. Not until she'd tossed that golden brown hair over her shoulder and announced that she had a date. With a man who had dumped her, no less. A man she *should* have been wary of.

Gage's brow furrowed into a scowl with the thought. Then, as he approached the only major intersection in town, his foot went automatically to the brake. The light was green, but he stopped anyway. There were no other drivers behind him to get annoyed at the delay—no one was venturing out in Little Beach's latest torrential downpour without a good reason. For a brief moment, he wondered what *his* reason for being out and about was. Then he decided that his motives didn't stand up to questioning. He'd been making a nuisance of himself at the homes of various friends for the last two hours—ever since Jenny Oliver had laid the news on him that she had a date . . . ever since he had realized that the news bothered him.

He scowled again and turned suddenly onto Oceanside Drive instead of heading straight on the road that would have taken him home. He drove aimlessly until he came upon Timber House, clinging like a sodden old dowager to the edge of a cliff. The sight of the rustic old building might have surprised him had he not suspected that some small part of him had been headed there all along. The inn wasn't a place that he particularly wanted to be, but restless energy churned inside him and he knew that there was nowhere else to go but home. For the first time in recent memory, that thought didn't appeal to him.

He turned into the nearly empty parking lot and cruised through it slowly, his fingers playing a tense tattoo on the steering wheel. There was only a handful of cars to make a pathetic attempt at filling up the spaces. But, then, the weather was horrendous. Six weeks ago, under the same conditions, there wouldn't have been any cars there at all. Six weeks ago, Jenny Oliver hadn't been running dinner specials. She was making a difference, he admitted to himself with grudging admiration. She was smart and not afraid to take chances. Just as he had once been. Before Abby, before Oregon. Vague stirrings of envy twisted inside him with the thought, stirrings that made him want to roll up his shirt sleeves again and get back to the intoxicating challenge of going for all the marbles. Stirrings that woke up an elemental sense of competition inside him. No, *she* woke up a sense of competition inside him. More and more lately he found himself wanting to best her, to lock horns with her and find out who could save Timber House first, to bandy ideas about with her and drive her—and himself—to new heights, to new achievements. Damn her! What was she doing to him? What demons was she waking up inside him?

Stupid question. He had asked it of himself a hundred times lately and always got the same answer, one that he didn't like much. He swore softly and wrenched hard on the steering wheel, taking the car in an abrupt U-turn. It was time to go home, time to go back to the motives and purposes that had brought him to Little Beach in the first place, before he forgot what they were.

Then, as he turned into the aisle directly banking the hotel, he spotted her car. Bright red and gleaming from the rain, the 280 SL was the most perfect vintage Mercedes he had seen in a while. He had been forced to admit to himself sometime before that the car's sporty lines suited her. It was more classic than fancy, more stylish than ostentatious. It occurred to him, though he wanted to deny it, that Abby would never have been content with a thirteen-year-old car like Jenny's. The more he knew of Jenny Oliver, the more sure he was that the two women had little in common.

Little, he reminded himself harshly, but enough. He wasn't going to get burned by a woman like her again. Still, a small part of him scoffed at the thought and he found himself swerving abruptly into the next available parking space. Without giving himself a chance to think about what he was doing, he grabbed a newspaper from the seat beside him. Holding it over his head, he jumped from the car and made a dash for the shelter of the porte cochere.

He told himself that he just wanted to find out why she was still at the inn. Had the guy stood her up? Or had she just flown into wary flight and decided that she'd be safer at home with those boring television shows? Maybe she'd worked late instead and was just now wrapping things up to go home. Gage scowled. He shouldn't give a damn. What she did with her nights was none of his business.

The thought made him hesitate in the lobby. If he had any sense, he'd turn right around and go home, he thought. It probably wasn't too late to have dessert with the kids, and Mrs. Bastian would be itching to leave. Instead, he took the elevator up to the fifth floor, frowning again when he found it dark and deserted. There wasn't any telltale light coming from beneath Jenny's office door, but he knocked anyway.

No answer. He opened the door a crack and peered inside at empty darkness. Turning on his heel, he slammed the door and headed back for the elevator.

So the guy had picked her up here, he thought. That made sense. She'd probably be returning later for her car. Much too late for him to consider hanging around. He casually ignored the way the muscles in his shoulders tensed in frustration as he rode the elevator down to the lobby again.

Then his churning thoughts broke off suddenly. The elevator doors groaned open slowly under the weight of their age and he spotted her. He stepped slowly into the lobby, his watchful eyes following her as she came out of the rest room and headed toward the dining room.

She'd changed into a soft, gray suit after he had left her earlier. It was one that she'd worn before, and it had caught his attention then, too. Instead of exactly matching the color of her eyes, it seemed to lend them a blue shade. Her posture was erect and unrelenting as she made her way across the room, but it couldn't belie the energy simmering in her walk . . . or her femininity. Damn her femininity! Did she know that she was beautiful? he wondered. No, probably not. There wasn't a self-conscious bone in her body. Her clothes were businesslike and unrevealing, as though she didn't know that she had anything to show off . . . and only made him consider more the suggestion of firm, uptilted breasts and the narrow waist beneath them. The dark, burnished

gold of her hair seemed to glimmer beneath the antique chande-
lier overhead. He found himself studying the phenomenon as
though it could offer him some insight into the first woman who
had managed to unsettle him in five years. A woman who, to add
insult to injury, was one he couldn't afford to become interested
in. Involving himself with Jenny Oliver would mean making a
mockery of his life. He turned his back on the sight of her and
moved toward the door again decisively.

Four steps later, he stopped.

Jenny never looked in the direction of the elevator as she left
the rest room; she had no reason to. Yet some deep, inner part of
her seemed to detect his presence. The little hairs on the back of
her neck pricked up long before she glanced around. And why
not? she thought wildly. That intense, blue-black gaze had been
haunting her for two weeks. She was simply developing anten-
nae for it.

Even as she stopped and turned around, she knew that she
wasn't being paranoid. She knew that she would find Gage
Pierce in the lobby just as well as she knew that she would find
Colby Barrett waiting for her when she went back to their table in
the dining room.

And she was right.

She spotted him standing a few feet away from the elevator.
Her heart lurched strangely as their eyes met. Even at that
distance, she couldn't miss the sparkling, silent challenge in his
gaze. She forced herself to nod at him disinterestedly and turn
away. To her credit, the sudden flutter of her heart never revealed
itself on her face. She made her way calmly into the dining room,
wordlessly dismissing his presence, but her thoughts churned
chaotically.

What was he doing here? And why on earth did she care that
he had come back anyway? Because of that look in his eyes, she
answered herself, her thoughts racing. Because he was up to
something again . . . and that something concerned her, just as it
always did. Or did it concern the hotel? He'd thought she had a
date. Was that why he was coming back to the inn so late,
assuming that she wouldn't be there, that she'd be having dinner

in Longport City? Did he have something up his sleeve, something that concerned International?

No. No, that was ridiculous. She was being paranoid. What could he possibly be doing that would concern International? Making copies of the books? Swiping them to show them to the conglomerate honchos? That was stupid. The tycoons at International already knew that Timber House was on its knees. They didn't want the business. They wanted a piece of prime, ocean-front land, complete with natural rock jetties that formed a secluded beach cove. They didn't care about what sort of profit the hotel might or might not be turning. They cared only about what they could build in its place after they tore it down. No, Gage wasn't here because he had hatched some sort of plot with International.

He was here because she was.

A strange surge of excitement coursed through her. Her knees felt oddly shaky as she finally slid into her chair across the table from Colby.

"Something wrong?" he asked solicitously, pouring her some wine. He'd been very solicitous that night. She found his manner oddly irritating—and stale after her spicy bouts with Gage.

"You look like you've seen a ghost," he went on.

"In a manner of speaking," Jenny muttered absently, her eyes drifting nervously back to the lobby. A demented one, she added to herself. And he was haunting her. Oh, yes, he was haunting her. She had to stifle the beginnings of a wild, nervous laugh.

Colby was studying her curiously. "Well, this place must have a few," he answered, easily adapting to the new turn their conversation had taken. One of the traits he'd developed in the last few years was a smoothness that went well with his looks . . . looks that hadn't deteriorated as she had so childishly hoped.

Jenny glanced up at him blankly, her thoughts still reeling. "A few of what?" she asked, forcing a polite smile.

Colby scowled. "Ghosts. I was saying that I suppose the place is old enough to have a few."

"Well, it's old enough to have a few fine traditions, at any rate." The slow, rusty voice ripped into their conversation suddenly and rubbed against Jenny's raw nerves like sandpaper.

He had followed her.

Even though she had known with some small instinctive part of her that he would, she still nearly choked on her wine. She coughed slightly, then placed her glass unsteadily back onto the table. Her startled eyes flew up to meet Gage's.

Oh, God, she thought wildly, there was that smile again. So self-satisfied, so pleased with himself. He was going to make trouble. He was going to try to rattle her.

"What . . . traditions?" she said softly.

"I was thinking about the one regarding this outstanding table by the sea window." His grin widened as he glanced down at their table. "You know, how it's always been reserved for the Oliver family."

It was. That was why she had chosen it for Colby and herself. It was the best table in the house, and had always been reserved for her family. But why would Gage point that out? Alarm bells began to sound in the back of her brain just as he turned away from her to call out to a passing waiter.

"Excuse me, Robert. I think we need another place setting here."

Jenny gaped at him for full seconds before she was able to find her voice. "You can't do this," she breathed as understanding finally dawned on her.

"Of course I can, Jenny Oliver. It's tradition," he answered softly. There was no doubt that his words were meant for her alone. His voice was more soft and sultry than she had ever heard it, and it excluded Colby as though he had sectioned the table off with a brick wall. Jenny felt a slight shiver touch her skin, but it wasn't brought on by any kind of chill. She was feeling hot again. Very hot. She pulled surreptitiously and nervously at the collar of her blouse as she fought to regain her composure.

"Not for you, it's not," she managed to say after a moment. "You're not an Oliver."

"Ah, but I am an owner. Same difference, wouldn't you say?"

Their voices were hushed, but vibrant with tension. Long after they had fallen silent, their gazes continued to hold with the same simmering energy.

For a moment, his held her mesmerized. Then she shook her

head fiercely, breaking loose of the spell. "No! I wouldn't!" she snapped, her voice louder now.

His only response was to sit down next to her. He draped his arm casually over the back of her chair in an oddly possessive gesture that she didn't have time to analyze. The brush of his arm against her shoulders ignited all her defenses, and more strange, fluid heat. She caught her breath as she felt it coasting through her again—and lost enough precious seconds to sacrifice the battle. Before she could open her mouth again, Robert brought the extra place setting and Gage turned to Colby.

"Colby Barrett, isn't it? We met at a Jaycee's meeting a while back. You've got law offices over in Brookings, if I remember correctly."

Colby looked more than a little bit taken aback. Jenny looked stunned. He knew Colby. Of course, he would know Colby. They'd both been living on the small, cloistered island for years. She remembered telling him about her long-ago crush on the man and how it had ended, and closed her eyes weakly against a flood of embarrassment. She detested the thought of Gage Pierce knowing about any of her failures.

She didn't see Colby's eyes go from Gage to her and then back again before he answered. "Right. And you're Gage Pierce. Moved here a few years back from the East Coast, didn't you?"

"Everybody knows everybody in this godforsaken town," Jenny muttered, then opened her eyes and straightened abruptly in her chair. It would be much too easy to lean back against the warm support of Gage's sinewy arm.

"Gage is, uh, my partner," she supplied, desperate for some kind of explanation that would soothe Colby's obviously ruffled feathers. She had discovered an hour ago that she didn't much care for him anymore, but manners were manners, after all. "Although not by any choice of my own," she went on, wondering distantly if she were babbling. "Ed sold a portion of the—"

"Half," Gage corrected her. "As in fifty percent."

His voice was warm, even idle, but only on the surface. Beneath it there was a trace of laughter as he enjoyed provoking her again. Jenny wondered wildly if she was the only one who could hear it. She slanted a hostile look at him but didn't dare argue with him. Not now. Later. Later she would get her revenge when she bought the whole thing out from under him.

"As I was saying," she continued smoothly, "my father sold half of Timber House to Gage a few months ago."

Colby downed the remainder of his wine in one aggressive swallow. "I'd heard something to the effect that Ed was trying to drum up cash to keep the place on its feet," he responded, his eyes intent on Gage. "I'm glad to learn that someone was able to oblige him. I think I speak for the entire town when I say that I'd like to see Timber House saved. I don't, however, think this is the time or the place to discuss it. Don't you agree, Mr. Pierce?"

"*I* do," Jenny jumped in pointedly.

Gage lazily raised an eyebrow at her. "Oh, so do I," he agreed too smoothly, too innocently.

She knew he was up to something, but she had no choice but to take the bait. She had to get him out of there.

"Good," she replied sweetly. "Then we can discuss whatever it is you're here to discuss with me tomorrow morning. I'll be in my office by eight." She leaned back in her chair, making it clear that she was waiting for him to leave.

Then that satisfied, slow grin touched his lips again and her heart plummeted down into her toes. She knew in a flash that leaving was the last thing he intended to do, no matter how firmly and coolly she tried to insinuate that he should.

"There's nothing particular I want to discuss with you, Jenny Oliver," he responded in a virtual whisper, his eyes snagging hers again.

Jenny felt suddenly light-headed with a furious surge of anger. How could he—why *would* he—want to do this to her? He couldn't know that she was bored with Colby. Her pride wouldn't *let* him know. He couldn't be trying to save her from a hopelessly tiresome date. He was trying to rattle her. Again.

"Then what the—" she began hotly, but he cut her off.

"Temper, temper," he cautioned maddeningly. "I merely stopped by for something to eat." As though to prove his point, he reached past her for a menu.

"There's a diner six blocks into town," she bit out.

He kept his gaze on the menu, a distracted frown forming between his eyes. "But the food's better here," he answered. "Especially after you dumped the old chef and hired that new guy."

A soft, warm smile inched its way onto her face at his subtle compliment, but she bit her lip against it. She was *not* going to allow herself to be buoyed by the vague appreciation she heard in his voice. She wouldn't let her train of thought be deferred to another track again simply because he suddenly, uncharacteristically, decided to show her some approval.

"Fine," she answered tightly. "So enjoy it at one of the other sixteen empty tables. I happen to be using this one."

He dropped his menu onto the table again with a small smile, then pushed his chair back. "What's the matter, Jenny Oliver?" he teased. "Getting rattled again?"

"Don't flatter yourself!"

"Too bad. I rather like it when you get rattled. You get this wild look about you. A decidedly sexy wild look."

For a brief moment, she was rendered speechless by his comment. Sexy? This man didn't talk about sexy. He talked about partnership agreements. He didn't talk about things bathed in warmth; he talked of things steeped in ice. She swallowed convulsively, not at all sure how to deal with this new side of him. Fresh heat took her by storm, leaving her feeling shaken.

"You—" she began, but then he cut her off.

"Excuse me a moment. If Robert returns before I get back, would you do me a favor and order me a steak? Medium rare should be fine. I won't be long."

Her fury was so sudden and so all-encompassing that it almost choked her. She jumped to her feet as well, but it quickly became evident that Gage didn't intend to wait around for her response. Before she was even able to find her voice, he was leaving the dining room, disappearing around the corner into the lobby.

"Damn you!" she snapped, oblivious to Colby's startled look. "Oh, damn you! You did it again." Galvanized by the frustrated anger that burned through her, she started after him.

Adopting a little half jog, half walk, she was able to catch up with him right outside the rest rooms. She was too irritated to think about what she was doing. She completely forgot that she didn't want to touch him until it was too late. She reached out and clutched at his arm with such force that he almost fell into her.

The abrupt end to his momentum tampered with her balance as well, and after an initial moment of surprise, he reached out to steady her. His arm slid firmly and supportively around her waist as he pulled her against him.

It happened so rapidly that neither of them completely realized what they were doing. Jenny reached up impulsively to hold onto him, and the primitive sexuality that she had first sensed in him that day in the elevator became suddenly real and tangible. His arms were hard and sturdy around her . . . so male. So strong. The feel of him made her senses spin and her skin feel even more flushed than it ever had before. The electricity that she had seen so often in his gaze was suddenly alive. It was in his touch. It was hot, and it seared its way clear through to her bones where his hands touched her waist. It burned through the thin fabric of her blouse where her breasts pressed against his chest. It stunned her. She glanced up at him quickly and saw a strange, smoldering understanding in his eyes.

She gasped softly, then wrenched away from him, her first instinct being to flee from what she had seen, from what she had felt. Feeling was notorious for dropping the short straw in one's lap. Feeling like this was lethal.

"Don't . . . touch me. Please," she whispered raggedly. She stood stiffly, trying to catch her breath, her fists clenched at her sides.

"You'd rather have fallen on your face?" Gage responded, but his voice fell far short of its usual mockery. They'd both felt it then, she thought wildly. She hadn't imagined it.

She scrambled to regain her anger. It seemed the safest recourse now by far. "I'd rather know why you're doing this to me," she answered, her voice still vaguely tremulous. "What are you doing here? What are you trying to accomplish?"

In the time it had taken her to speak, Gage seemed to have recovered himself. He *had* felt what had happened to them when they had touched; she was sure of it. But she was equally sure that he, too, had decided that it was best to ignore it. The realization both bothered and steadied her, making it easier for her to remember that she was angry.

He offered her a tiny frown and glanced over his shoulder at the men's-room door. "What am I trying to accomplish?" he repeated. "You really want an answer?"

She was struggling too hard to regain her poise to realize that she was stepping into one of his traps. "You're damned right I do," she ground out.

He sighed too dramatically. "How do I say this politely?" he murmured. "Okay, how's this? I'm trying to take care of a common bodily need, the urgency of which is becoming increasingly important, so if you'll excuse me—"

Amazement whitened her already pale skin even more. "A common—" she began to sputter incredulously. Then words failed her. Before she could collect herself, Gage shrugged and pushed through the men's-room door.

"You asked," he tossed back over his shoulder.

She actually gave serious thought to following him. Perhaps if she could have held onto her anger, she might have. But even while her pulse raced and her breath came quickly and furiously, she gradually became aware of the fact that people were watching. She colored fiercely and ducked her head, feeling suddenly overwhelmed.

She didn't know how he was able to do this to her. She didn't know how to prevent it. She was scared.

"Ms. Oliver?" The maître d's voice brought her head up again abruptly. She blinked at the man in distracted panic.

"Yes?"

"The gentleman with whom you and Mr. Pierce were dining . . . he left this for you." After a moment of embarrassed hesitation, he continued: "He paid the bar tab as well." Then the maître d' handed Jenny a small, folded message.

"Mr. Pierce and I were *not*—" she began heatedly, then broke off, desperately struggling for composure again. "Thank you, Martin," she finished coolly, then made her way back into the dining room again.

She slid into her chair and unfolded the note. Within seconds, fresh anger began to grip her as she read it.

It is quite obvious that I've intruded upon something a little more volatile than professional tension between two partners. I leave you to battle things out with Mr. Pierce without the distraction of my presence. No hard feelings. I think you're worth competing for, but next time we eat in Longport City.

Colby

She closed her eyes weakly. He wouldn't call her again, despite his polite assurances. She was oddly, tremendously, relieved. But she didn't want to feel relieved. She wanted to feel furious with Gage Pierce for making a sideshow out of her date. Instead, she was furious with him because he was able to break through her protective, cool shield and play hell with her composure time and time again, when no one else could. When no one else had been able to in nearly nine years. When she thought she knew better than to let that shield be broken.

"Shall we order?" Gage asked conversationally as he arrived back at the table. He folded his hard, lean body into the chair beside hers, then reached for his napkin, snapping it open with a flick of his wrist. Jenny's gray eyes darkened like thunderclouds as she watched him.

"I'm not hungry enough to put up with you as a dinner partner," she answered, her voice dangerously soft. I don't want to put up with you as a dinner partner, she thought silently. I don't dare.

Infuriatingly, he ignored her. "Where's your friend?"

She raised her hand and crumbled Colby's note with deadly calm, then opened her palm to drop it unceremoniously into the ashtray. "Gone. He didn't want to intrude. Why did you do it?"

He lifted his eyebrows at her too innocently. "I didn't ask him to leave."

"You didn't have to," she snapped. "You chased him away quite well. You know, I can understand a little professional friction between us—there are numerous possible reasons for it. I don't want to sell to International—you do. I hold staff meetings after working hours; you hold them during the prime hours of the day. As I said, there are numerous reasons for it. I can't, however, understand why you would want to play havoc with my personal life."

She had more than suspected that he wouldn't answer her, but his obvious avoidance of her accusation was more than she could take. "Pass me the wine, would you?"

She pushed the wine bucket at him abruptly, then grabbed her purse. "Here. It's all yours. I'm leaving."

She was halfway to her feet before his smoldering dark eyes snagged hers again. Even as he trapped her in his gaze, he poured fresh wine into her glass, as though challenging her to stop him. Oh, God, those eyes, she thought, sinking weakly back into her chair again. The same current of sexuality that she had felt before seemed to reach out and touch her once more. It left her feeling hot, weak, and incapable of speech. She was suddenly grateful for the support of the chair.

His eyes finally left hers to study the label on the bottle. "Good wine. Nice choice. Your's or Barrett's?"

She stared at him for a moment, her pulse throbbing in her throat. "Mine," she answered eventually, shortly.

He nodded appreciatively before his eyes came back to her. "Don't waste it," he cautioned in the rusty growl that she was coming to know so well.

A brief, burning shiver ripped through her. "Why?" she managed to ask softly. "Why shouldn't I waste it?" Her words were defiant; her voice was not. Burgeoning panic kept her from reaching her full potential for flippancy this time.

Why, indeed? Gage asked himself silently, doubting his sanity for the hundredth time in an hour. Because he, Gage Pierce, was a weak man? And because he always went after what he wanted, whether it was good for him or not? Because she had looked so damnably beautiful in the candlelight, and it had infuriated him to watch a suave, pretentious pretty boy enjoying the fire in those quicksilver eyes? Or because he knew Colby Barrett and knew, too, that Jenny Oliver was a woman who deserved more—who needed more—than candy-coated responses and genteel lies? Because he could give that to her and didn't dare?

But he didn't say the words aloud. "It's getting late," he said instead. "We're here. We might as well eat."

He was right. Or was he? Was she simply looking for an excuse to stay awhile longer? She didn't want to think about it. She was afraid to think about it. Instead, she watched him guardedly and reached for the menu.

She had just picked up her wine again when he spoke once more. "So tell me, what is it about me that you detest so much? The fact that I'm a man, not a calculator?" His tone was lazy; his words were not. "I suppose a man like Colby Barrett comes very close to being a calculator. Mechanical answers, concise lines. Is that why you preferred having dinner with him to having dinner with me? Because you feel safe with him and detest me?"

The heavy lashes that shadowed her cheeks flew up just as she had begun to relax again. Her mouth dropped open as she stared at him. Detest him? Have dinner with him? she thought wildly, incredulously. She respected his intelligence and dreaded his smile; she crumbled time and time again to the powers of those haunting eyes . . . but detest him? No. Hardly. If she detested him, she wouldn't have anything to be frightened of, she wouldn't have any reason to fight him. But she *was* frightened of him, frightened of what he could do to her, and fighting him came naturally.

She cleared her throat carefully. "I . . . I don't understand," she answered, her voice thin.

"We've been circling each other like two wild beasts for weeks. Surely you've noticed."

"Oh, I've noticed," she muttered.

"My question is: Why?" He posed the question smoothly, as though she hadn't said anything.

Jenny swallowed back her surprise. "Well, I can assure you that it has nothing to do with your not being a calculator," she replied jauntily, hoping her tone would carry the lie. It seemed to. She gathered a bit of confidence as he lifted a brow at her.

"Are you playing with me again?" she demanded suddenly, surprising even herself. "For God's sake, Gage! You walked in here with a chip on your shoulder the first day we met, and you haven't dropped it since! You've spent two weeks sneaking along behind me like you were my self-appointed nemesis! After what you did to me tonight, how can you possibly sit there and ask me a question like that?"

"Self-appointed nemesis," he drawled. "Well, that's progress, I suppose. It's a hell of a lot more flattering than the 'demented ghost' line." A small smile touched his lips as he watched her flush again.

She tried to ignore it. "Furthermore," she went on, gaining momentum, "even if you had floated in here like a cherub that first day, I would have gotten my dander up when I found out who you were. I was shocked to find Timber House in the condition it's in, and I blame you—and Ed—for letting it get this way. You were his partner, damn it! You could have done something! Why did you even bother to buy into the place if you didn't care about it?" she demanded.

"And you do?" he shot back. Oddly, he wasn't sure if he was really angry at her accusation, or if he was just enjoying sparring with her again. Her skin was rosy, her eyes bright, as she allowed the conversation to get to her.

She *was* beautiful, he decided. At least when she was angry.

"What?" she demanded, bracing her elbows on the table and leaning toward him slightly. Her silver eyes flashed fire.

"Care about the hotel," he clarified, watching her musingly.

"Of course I do! Would I be here instead of in San Francisco if I didn't?"

"I don't know, Jenny Oliver. Suppose you tell me. You obviously weren't concerned with the condition of Timber House during all those years you stayed away." He continued to watch her intently, not taking his eyes off her even while the waiter delivered their meals.

Jenny picked at her prime rib distractedly, trying to hold on to her temper. "My father and I never saw eye to eye on a lot of things," she explained tightly. "We lived together in the same house for twenty years—my mother died when I was born—but we were strangers to each other. He was . . . sort of a loner. He was stubborn and always did things his way. Timber House was one of those things. Even if I had still lived in Little Beach and made suggestions regarding the inn, he wouldn't have listened to me now any more than he listened to me when I was thirteen and tried to tell him that one of the desk clerks was robbing us blind. The desk clerk, by the way, got away with almost seventeen thousand dollars. By the time Ed admitted that I was right, she was long gone."

Gage's eyes were contemplative now, but still intent. "Is that why you left?" he asked. She had the wildest, craziest impression that a great deal depended on her answer.

"Because Ed was stubborn and pig-headed?" she clarified warily. She thought about it a minute, absently taking another bite of her beef only to discover that she was hungrier than she had thought. She took yet another bite, stalling while she tried to formulate an answer.

"Well, I can't deny that Ed had *something* to do with my leaving the island," she answered eventually, watching Pierce carefully over the rim of her glass as she took another sip of wine. "I spent more time here when I was a kid than I did at home or school, I think. And I developed a passion for the workings of a hotel. I'd absorbed a lot of knowledge over the course of those years, and I wanted to use it. I wanted to work here—I would have been happy doing anything from cooking to cleaning to managing—but Ed wouldn't let me. He told me that Timber House was his turf, and that he wasn't going to let any kid of his tell him what to do with it. He knew me better than I thought he did, I guess. He knew that given half a chance, I'd have every standard operation turned upside down while I tried to find a better, more profitable way." She paused to shrug and smile sheepishly.

"Anyway," she went on, "I eventually realized that the only way I was ever going to be able to work for a hotel was to leave Little Beach and Timber House. So I went to San Francisco, found a hotel there, and worked my way up in the ranks. I guess you could say that it was my bid for all the marbles. I ran away, and I ran fast, although no one chased me. In retrospect, I'd have to say that it worked out for the best. Fate, I suppose."

Gage's eyes thinned speculatively again, but Jenny didn't

notice. She finished her prime rib and sat back with a satisfied sigh.

"Did you find them? All the marbles?" he asked abruptly.

"What? Oh, the marbles. Sure. In a place like San Francisco, they're there for the taking if you want them badly enough. And I did. I was also lucky enough to lay siege to the finest hotel in the city when I was looking for my first job." Suddenly, she laughed brightly. "I didn't know Warwick Towers from the Budget Inn! I just picked the place out of the telephone book because it was closest to the apartment I'd rented! Can you believe that?"

He did. Especially the part about her laying siege to the hotel in order to get the job. He didn't doubt that for a minute. She'd be a hard person to refuse once she'd made up her mind that she wanted something.

He watched her carefully as she sighed and leaned back in her chair. She tossed her hair over her shoulder with a little shake of her head and ran a long, manicured fingernail under the collar of her blouse—a gesture he knew meant that she was nervous. He tried to deny the surge of curiosity that rose in him as he waited for her to finish.

"Well, anyway, I've never regretted leaving, if that's what you're asking," she went on eventually. "It's nice to be back, but I wouldn't trade those years in California for anything in the world. I learned a lot." She paused, then frowned. "And I . . . grew up a lot. You can make a business do just about whatever you want it to, but you can't do the same thing with people. It took me a long time to learn that." She looked up at him suddenly, sharply . . . and pointedly. It was almost as though she were accusing him of something. Gage found himself getting defensive without even knowing why he was doing it.

"Nice to be back." He repeated her words with a strange, almost sarcastic edge, she thought. Her eyes narrowed as she watched him.

"Well, yes. Little Beach is . . . quaint. It's not a bad town. And it was home for a long time."

"Most people visit home once in a while," he pointed out, "no matter how far away they wander. You didn't."

Yes, she had been right. He was being sarcastic and hard again, just as he had been when they had been discussing Colby earlier. She didn't understand now any more than she had then. Frustration washed over her, making her voice sound clipped.

"I would have, given half a chance."

"Then why didn't you?" It was a demand. She felt her temper twitching.

"Because Ed had a magical way of discouraging visits, especially during the last few years. That's why," she snapped, suddenly remembering the hurt as freshly as if it had happened yesterday. Why was she allowing him to do this to her, to make her relive it? How was he *able* to do this to her? She hated him for it, yet felt driven to explain.

"It was always subtle," she went on bitterly. "I never knew whether he planned it that way or not. But whenever I was free to fly up, he wasn't going to be in town. Or he was going to be busy all weekend. You'll forgive me if I tell you that I saw no reason to fly back up here if he wasn't going to be around. He did come to San Francisco twice, but both times were over five years ago and it was only to see a banker friend of his, not me, although I think we managed to have lunch or dinner together or something. And that was it. Now that you know the fascinating story of Ed and Jenny Oliver, do you think you could lay off?"

Gage's eyes narrowed. His voice was vaguely assessing again. "Ed never went out of town over the course of the last few years," he answered slowly. "That is, with the minor exception of visiting the hospital in Portland."

"Are you calling me a liar?" She straightened in her chair, furious.

"No," he answered in a level tone. "I'm just wondering why *he* lied."

At first she looked startled. "To who?"

"To you."

"About not planning to be here when I was visiting? Did he?"

"If he told you that, yes. He rarely left the island."

She shrugged deliberately. Her muscles protested stiffly as she tried to force them into a nonchalant reflex. "Oh, hell, I don't know. Maybe he just thought it was easier to lie than to admit that he had no burning desire to see me."

He was sorry for his words the minute he saw the pain flash across her face, the second her retort came back so sharp and defensive. Regret twisted in him with shocking immediacy. Yet his guilt—and a sudden sense of frustration—had the adverse effect of making his voice more accusing. He had to find out. He had to know just who this woman was . . . and there was only one way she would react enough to talk to him. He had to rattle her.

"He had cancer," Gage pointed out tersely.

"So I'm told," Jenny responded hollowly.

"But you didn't know it then."

"No, I didn't! He never told me!"

Her voice shattered the escalating tension in the air between them. It rang out with anger . . . and something else. He thought about it a moment, then identified it. Hurt. Pain. As clear as it had been in her eyes a moment before. He scowled—and suddenly was sure beyond a shadow of a doubt that she was telling the truth. Ed hadn't encouraged her to visit. And he hadn't told her that he was sick. Whatever his reasons had been, Ed Oliver's estrangement from his daughter had been more his doing than hers.

A strange sense of satisfaction filled him, but he brushed it aside quickly, angrily. So what if Ed had, intentionally or not, painted her black for reasons that no one would ever know? That might justify the fact that he liked her. But it didn't justify the fact that his blood quickened when he watched her walk across a room, her skirt swirling softly around long coltish legs. It didn't justify the fact that he'd felt a hard, undeniable tightening inside him when she had fallen into his arms. It didn't justify the fact that she made him think about all sorts of things that he hadn't thought about in a long time . . . and didn't dare think about again.

Gage swore beneath his breath and drained his wine, trying to get a grip on his churning feelings. So he liked her. That was okay. He could live with that. But he couldn't live with wanting her.

He deposited his wineglass on the table again with a decisive tap, intending to leave. The night had gone on long enough. It shouldn't have come this far in the first place, he thought. But her voice caught him just as he was about to push back his chair. He found himself filling both of their glasses again.

"Anyway, what about you?" she asked, prompting him with a soft smile that threatened to wash away the last of his resolve. Yes, her smile was soft, he thought, but it was also tremulous. She hadn't liked their topic of conversation, not at all. And she was determined to guide them away from it, he realized. But she intended to do it with dignity.

"What's your story?" she pushed, sensing another of his brooding withdrawals. "You weren't born here. Colby said that you moved here a few years ago. From where? And whatever induced you to buy into Timber House?"

"You mean because I obviously don't care about the place?" he asked. His voice was challenging again, and somewhat defensive. Before she had a chance to respond, he went on: "I cared about Ed, not the hotel. A widower, his daughter off in parts unknown . . . he was alone, and doing his damnedest to keep this place going. He wouldn't believe that it couldn't be saved. I admired him as much as I felt sorry for him. He needed cash, so I gave it to him in the only way he would accept it. I bought into the place. He was too proud to accept a loan."

"That's it? You didn't do it because you thought you could turn around and sell to International?" The words were out before she could stop them, before she even knew that she was going to ask them. It was something that had been hounding her since the day he had first walked into her office. Part of her wanted to trust him, and part of her didn't dare. Part of her wanted to hear his answer, and part of her simply needed to believe the worst of him.

The gaze he turned on her was thunderously dark. "Is that what you think?" he asked quietly.

Her heart crowded her throat, but she forced herself to nod. "You knew he had cancer," she pointed out, her chin lifting slightly, defiantly. He tried not to notice.

"I also knew that when he died, you would be my new partner. I read the contracts I sign. Meticulously," he responded with gritty bluntness.

Jenny flinched slightly, but persisted. She had come this far. She had to know. "You also thought that I'd be willing to sell to

International, that I'd be more willing than Ed to give up on a lost cause."

His eyes held hers, dark and challenging as always. "That's right," he answered.

"So?" she demanded. "Is that why you bought in? To turn a huge profit somewhere down the road?"

"Does it matter, Jenny Oliver?" His tone was deliberately neutral. "What difference does it make if I was helping a friend or trying to make some money? Both intentions are human and at least somewhat honorable."

Her breath was a solid mass in her throat, immovable. She wasn't sure why his answer was so important, but it was. She didn't intend to let him slide out of it with more glib, enigmatic words.

"It matters," she whispered. "To me, anyway. I need to know . . ." She paused, searching for the right words. "I just wondered how human you really are. Tell me."

Several seconds passed before he answered. He watched her with a long, considering expression until she was sure that he had no intention of telling her. Then he looked away abruptly. "It's really a night for cleaning slates, isn't it?" he murmured. Then he added, "You already know the answer, Jenny Oliver. It's right there in that steel-trap brain of yours, if you look for it. But since it's late and we're both tired, I'll remind you anyway. Neither Ed nor I had ever heard of International when I bought into the hotel."

Jenny blinked at him in surprise. He was right. The relief that swam through her was so sudden, so strong, that it shocked her. And scared her. He was human. Underneath it all, he was a kind man, generous . . . and a pushover for stubborn old men. He'd spent five hundred thousand dollars on a hotel he didn't want just to help out an old man who had few friends and didn't know what to do with the ones he did have.

Why did that frighten her so?

Her fingers tightened on her wineglass, but she never had the chance to bring it to her lips again.

"Shall we go?" he asked abruptly.

She was too startled by his suggestion—and too willing to call an end to the disturbing night—to offer any objection. She nodded dully and reached for her purse. Their tentative truce had come to an end for the evening, and she had perhaps learned more about him than she had really wanted to know. She threw him a troubled look over her shoulder as she led the way out of the hotel, but he didn't seem to notice.

Then, as they left the porte cochere and stepped out under cloudy but somewhat more amenable skies, her consternation erupted into fluttering, instinctive panic. He touched her again.

His gesture was natural and appropriate. He simply reached out and took her elbow as they crossed the parking lot. But the touch of his strong fingers gripping her arm brought an almost familiar shiver of awareness to her and she nearly stumbled. Her thoughts spun away from her as though they had never existed.

"Come on," he directed her quietly, "I'll walk you to your car."

She tried instinctively to pull away from him. His touch was not something that she wanted to tangle with again, but his hold on her was too tight. "It's right here," she snapped, attacking him with words as a last resort to get him to release her. "You know, if you have some latent caveman fantasies, you might try dragging me by the hair. It might hurt less."

Still, he didn't let her go. Instead, he pulled her abruptly around to face him, pinning her between her car and his hard body so quickly that her breath escaped her in a little burst. The familiar shiver of awareness deep inside her turned into the burning heat that she was also beginning to know too well. She stared into his eyes, her own wide. Her pulse danced with dizzying speed.

"You're playing hell with me. Do you know that?" His voice was deep and smooth. Not seductive. At least it wasn't what most women would hear as seduction. Jenny heard honesty . . . and the most astounding vulnerability. From him? Her breath caught in her throat as she met his eyes. She felt herself beginning to tremble.

"I—" she began, but he cut her off more completely than he could have with words. He released her elbow and framed her face with his strong hands in an uncharacteristically tender

72

gesture. His eyes burned into hers. Jenny froze, stunned at the thought that he would touch her so.

"You're the brightest flame I've come across in a long time," he went on roughly. "And as far as moths go, I keep getting weaker and weaker. I've got to do this, you know. I'll regret it ten minutes from now, but I've got no choice. You don't leave me one."

It was the only warning she had, and it wasn't enough. He was talking riddles again, and even as she struggled to comprehend his words, his mouth found hers and she simply didn't have the power to fight him. A thunderbolt of electricity passed between them instantly. Once he touched his lips to hers, she couldn't pull away.

His lips parted hers forcefully. She wouldn't have expected his kiss to be any different, yet it shook her to the bottom of her toes. His tongue thrust its way into her mouth to challenge hers, just as his raven eyes had been challenging her for weeks.

The blood pounded in her brain as her hands found his shoulders and she clung to him. Her emotions whirled, at once protesting and giving in. He was so male, so virile. She felt her knees weaken as his mouth plundered hers, both hard and sweet at the same time. She knew that it was a turn of events that could prove perilous to her heart. She had known that from the start, but she still couldn't stop it from happening. She could feel herself drowning in him. Her pride was gone; her ego deserted her. Her heart thundered both in panic and wild excitement.

He crushed her to him, a savage intensity in his embrace. She knew suddenly that his strange words had been horribly honest —he would regret this, although she had no idea why. He held her as though he were a condemned man, and he moved his mouth over hers as though she could somehow save him.

And then, without warning, he released her.

He stepped away from her so suddenly that she barely had time to realize that he, too, was trembling slightly. She reached behind her quickly in an effort to steady herself with the door handle and stared at him speechlessly.

The smile he gave her was thin and strangely pained. "I was right," he murmured. "It was worth it. Good-bye, Jenny Oliver."

She brought a trembling hand to her lips as he walked away. They seemed to burn with the aftermath of his possession, so much so that she never even turned around when she heard the engine of his car roar to life and the wheels churn on the gravel parking lot. She simply stood there, stunned.

It took her a long time to comprehend the fact that Gage Pierce had actually kissed her. It took her even longer to realize that there had been something odd about the way he had said good-bye.

5

~~~~~~~~~~~~

He'd been wrong. It had taken him less than ten minutes to regret touching her. What was more, he couldn't seem to stop regretting it—or remembering that moment of weakness—as the days went by.

He just wasn't the sort of man who could make allowances for himself. He believed in taking responsibility for his actions, even impulsive ones, even crazy ones. And while kissing Jenny Oliver had easily been one of the craziest impulses he had ever succumbed to, he still couldn't let himself brush the memory of it under the carpet and forget about it. Mistakes came back to haunt a person that way. He knew that. And he knew that the only way to handle one was to analyze it, figure out where he went wrong, and make sure it never happened again.

That was precisely what he'd been doing in the days that had passed since he'd disrupted Jenny's dinner date. Analyzing. Figuring it out. Constantly.

The end result was that he had been irritable for days. Even Ben and Danny had noticed it. And what kind of an excuse could he offer two little boys? Tell them that their father had been impossible to live with because he'd met a woman who was driving him crazy, a woman who was strong and wild and man-shy and vulnerable, a woman he wanted—and who, worse still—he had also come to like a great deal? Even if they hadn't, at seven and ten years old, been much too young to understand the hell a woman could play with his soul, they'd never understand what such an attraction could do to their lives if their father succumbed to it. They were, thank God, too young really to remember the way it had been before. They were too young to understand the lengths he had gone to, the determination that had driven him, in his efforts to make sure that they—especially Danny—never had to go through that again.

He stepped down harder on the accelerator, veered his car around a corner, and swore softly. Jenny Oliver was getting to him. She was starting to play havoc with his soul, and he couldn't allow that to happen. Back in the beginning, when she'd first arrived at Timber House, he'd been smarter than he'd known. He'd believed what Ed had told him about his daughter. In a way, he'd clung to it. It was only after he'd begun to watch her and try to figure her out, that he'd started wondering if Ed really *had* led him to believe that Jenny was selfish and hard, that she didn't want any part of her father or Timber House. It was later that it had occurred to him that Ed really hadn't done anything but supply facts. Jenny had left Little Beach when she was twenty years old. She was a whiz at business management and had been catapulted to a prestigious position with one of the most well known hotels in the country almost overnight. She never came back to Little Beach. She'd never offered to try to help him save Timber House when it started its downhill slide. She didn't know that he had cancer, that he was dying.

And Gage had taken all of that, and had seen what he had wanted to see. Without knowing her, he'd supplied her motivations: she didn't help Ed; she didn't stay in touch with Ed, because she had brains for a heart and was selfish as well. He'd determined that she was another Abby, and was prepared to dislike her on sight.

Unfortunately, it hadn't happened that way. He'd *liked* her on sight . . . albeit grudgingly. He'd liked rattling her and arguing with her and watching her eyes burn. He liked watching her laugh and smile, scowl and think and push. He liked waiting for one of the tart little speeches she'd invariably succumb to when he teased her. He *liked* her.

And he wanted her.

But he couldn't allow himself to have her. It would have been easier than he'd originally thought—he'd been pleasantly shocked at the way she'd responded to his kiss—but he still couldn't allow himself to pursue her, to pursue *anything* with her. Not because she was all the things he'd originally thought . . . but because she wasn't.

He couldn't do that to himself. He was happy now, wasn't he? Much happier than he had been in New York. And Jenny Oliver would suck him right back into that maelstrom again. It would be New York all over again. For him, and for Danny. That was the worst part. Danny was the part that wouldn't let him risk it.

By the time he rang the doorbell of the large, shingled cottage that had once been Ed's, he'd recited the same litany to himself a thousand times, trying to convince himself of its merit. He knew what he was doing, he knew why he was doing it, and he knew that it was right.

He tried not to let himself remember that Danny didn't leave him much choice.

Jenny hadn't been able to bring herself to move into Ed's first-floor bedroom. It simply hadn't seemed right. She'd opted instead to store all of her father's personal possessions in there and seal it off. Her old bedroom on the second floor was more than adequate for her own needs. Although it was smaller and using it meant heating an additional floor, it had a wonderful view of the sea and she was comfortable there.

Unfortunately, the room was at the back of the house. When the doorbell rang just as she'd begun to dress, she didn't have the option of peeking out the window to see who was on the porch.

For the first time, she regretted that. She was pressed for time, and depending upon who it was, she was tempted to ignore their summons. If she had been any other kind of person, she might have ignored the bell anyway, but her curiosity wouldn't let her. Instead, she hurriedly fastened the last garter to her stockings, grabbed her bathrobe off the back of the door, and bounded down the stairs, shouting that she was coming.

She saw Gage even before she reached the last step. Her heart leaped crazily and she froze. It seemed to take her forever to tie the belt of her robe. Her fingers felt suddenly stiff, cold, and clumsy with panic.

Why on God's green earth had he come to her home?

The question slammed itself against the perimeters of her brain, making it nearly impossible for her to think of anything else, or even to move. Gage. Here, at her house. Why?

She took a deep, steadying breath and tried to force herself to be calm and rational. The truth of the matter was that his presence would have rattled her rather than shocked her a week before, but now it did both. Since he'd barged in on her dinner with Colby, he'd been avoiding her, obviously and determinedly. The contrast between his behavior lately and his old, brooding presence was stark.

But now he was standing on her porch, peering in at her with that slight smile and those watchful midnight eyes.

She swallowed hard, forcing herself to walk down the last few steps and open the door. She met his gaze straight on as she scrambled inwardly for composure, although it took every ounce of control she possessed.

Be sarcastic, she thought. Be flippant. Act decidedly unrattled. She cleared her throat.

"I'm only willing to fight with you at Timber House because I have no choice," she announced, her voice carefully dry. "I should warn you, however, that when it comes to invading my home, I have no intention of taking your games laying down. Try rattling me once, and you're out the door. I'm in charge of this turf—one hundred percent. No partners, no room for debate. Got it? Now, what do you want?"

For a moment, their eyes locked with the old, simmering challenge that they had always shared. They were both people who needed—who *demanded*—the upper hand, and usually got it. At the moment, she clearly possessed it. She could only wonder if he was going to allow her to keep it.

He didn't. He smiled, and her composure quickly became a thing of the past. She noticed his grin just as she finished speaking. Her heart skipped a beat. It spread over his face slowly, as though he didn't really intend it to be there but couldn't help himself. All thoughts of his motivations for being there fled from her mind as she stared at him. Smiling like that, he was the most naturally compelling man she had ever laid eyes on. A hot shiver tingled down her spine.

"Maybe you ought to give such a possibility some thought," he drawled. He pushed himself away from the porch post and sauntered toward her.

"Give . . . give what possibility some thought?" she asked uncertainly, still caught up in that smile.

His mouth twitched as though he were trying not to laugh. His dark eyes were suddenly merry. "The possibility of taking my games lying down," he supplied, his voice uncharacteristically provocative. "It might prove interesting."

Jenny stared at him blankly. His obvious meaning didn't occur to her immediately. Such a comment seemed so out of character for him that a part of her just stubbornly refused to accept it. Then understanding dawned on her and her eyes widened in surprise.

It took her an embarrassingly long time to recover. "Well, we're not going to find out. Go away," she finally managed. Her response was instinctive and panicked. Her palms felt suddenly clammy as she grabbed the doorknob again. She started to push the door closed impulsively.

"Oh, I intend to," he answered smoothly, blocking the door with his foot in a gesture that she was beginning to think was one of his major talents. He did it so successfully, so smoothly.

"Go away, that is," he finished. "I just dropped by to tell you so."

Another typical comment, cryptic and mysterious. He must hold the world's record for confusing people, she thought irritably, but she couldn't fight off her curiosity. She pulled the door open again.

"*What* did you just drop by to tell—" she started to prompt him in exasperation, but then she broke off. The moment she opened the door wide enough, he stepped past her into the foyer.

For a moment, she only stood there clutching the door handle as she stared after him, seething. He'd gotten the upper hand back again, all right, without half trying. He made his way calmly into the living room and had the nerve—or the stupidity—to drop down onto the sofa next to Chesterfield, the cat that had been Ed's. She slammed the door closed and followed him.

"I . . . uh . . . I wouldn't do that if I were you," she warned as he reached out to scratch the cat's ears. The huge gray tom was the one possession of Ed's that she hadn't been able to store away in his bedroom. That didn't stop her, however, from wishing daily that she had. He was a miserable excuse for a pet, sullen and independent, much like Ed himself. Unfortunately, unlike Ed, he was also nasty. Few people, with the possible exception of the old woman next door, were able to get near him without having their hands begin to resemble raw hamburger.

But Gage ignored her warning. He gave her a perfunctory glance for her efforts and proceeded to rub Chesterfield behind the ears. Apprehension twisted around Jenny's heart, although she couldn't for the life of her figure out why she should care if he got scratched or bitten. After all, she'd tried to warn him.

But her fears were premature. She watched, astounded, as Chesterfield let out a rumbling purr and rolled over on his back under Gage's ministrations, making it perfectly clear that he wanted his stomach tended to next.

"I don't believe it," she muttered, "although I don't suppose I should be surprised. Birds of a feather, and all that," she finished at his questioning look. "You can both be so cranky."

He ignored her sarcasm. "He must miss Ed. He's not usually so amenable."

"I know," Jenny responded drily.

"Have you been giving him salmon?"

"What?"

"Salmon," he explained with forced patience. "He likes salmon."

"Oh. Well, I suppose someone makes salmon-flavored cat food. I'll try to dig some up." She watched the pair dubiously. "Will it make him any easier to get along with?"

"Cat food won't," he predicted, hauling the massive cat onto his lap. Unbelievably, Chesterfield didn't protest the indignity of such treatment. "Ed used to run down to the docks every Friday night and get him fresh fish," Gage went on. "But salmon seems to be his favorite. I'd always bring some back with me on those rare occasions when I'd get over to Longport City."

"Salmon," Jenny repeated. She was having a hard time envisioning either him or Ed pampering a disagreeable old tomcat into submission. It seemed that the longer she stayed in Little Beach, the more human both men became . . . one who had rejected her love, and another she was determined not to give the same sort of chance to. It was disturbing and scary, something she wasn't at all sure she wanted to face.

She wasn't sure she wanted to share this lazy conversation with Gage Pierce, either. He had a way of turning the tables on her whenever she let her guard down with him. Her eyes narrowed slightly as she watched him. Was this some kind of a ploy, too, this talk of Ed and Chesterfield and salmon? Was he trying to lull her into a false sense of complacency before he pounced on her and rattled her again?

"What are you doing here?" She changed the subject abruptly and suspiciously. "I'm going to take a shot in the dark and guess that you didn't come over to tell me that the cat likes salmon. And while we're about it, I'm not too thrilled about the way you got in here, either. I don't appreciate being tricked into letting you inside."

Gage shrugged with a charming lack of innocence. "Who tricked you? You opened the door of your own volition. But either way, don't worry about it. It won't happen again."

It wasn't an apology. On the contrary, his words seemed designed to provoke the most curiosity in her. It worked.

"You know, this conversation is beginning to sound like a game of Clue. If you're trying to tell me something, then how about getting to it? I don't have time to play guessing games with you, Gage. I've got a six o'clock flight to catch, and I've got to get to the airport."

His response was a gaze that was both appreciative and frank. Her pulse fluttered uncomfortably as she watched his eyes rake over her. She took an uncertain step backward and frowned at him.

"It looks to be one hell of a flight," he drawled eventually. "Are you running off with Colby Barrett?"

"Colby? I . . ." she began, confused, then trailed off. Her voice sounded ragged and clearly flustered. Small wonder, she thought wildly. She watched his eyes as they slid boldly down her body, moving from her shoulders to her breasts before they finally riveted on the swell of her hips. She glanced down, following the trail of that ebony gaze.

And then she understood. She reached down and yanked her bathrobe closed again, tying the belt more securely with fingers that were suddenly trembling. Her robe had fallen open invitingly somewhere along the line, and the creamy ivory lace of her garters had been flashing out from the gap. Her blood pounded in her temples as she looked away from him, embarrassed and unable to meet his eyes any longer.

"Oh, damn!" she muttered helplessly.

Gage chuckled maddeningly. "Don't cover up on my account. I can't say that I mind the view."

Anger was the quickest and easiest way to cover her mortification. "If you want a show, then try one of the strip joints on the mainland," she snapped. "This one's over. My flight leaves in an hour and a half, and I *have* to get to San Francisco tonight. I've got to close down my apartment and tie up some loose ends, and tomorrow's the only day I can take away from Timber House. Fun's fun and all that, but you're going to have to leave."

He continued to grin at her nerve-wrackingly. "Go to the airport like that, and they'll hold the flight for you," he murmured. "If I were the pilot, I would."

Her heart turned over weakly at his response. She stared at him incredulously. She didn't know this man. This wasn't the brooding, watchful presence who had been shattering the orderly routine of her days at the inn. That Gage Pierce simply didn't talk like this. A slow, suffusing warmth claimed her and she turned away from him abruptly.

"Go home," she tried again, her voice breathless even as she struggled for her old flippancy. "Go do whatever it is you do when you're not bothering me."

She hurried into the kitchen, illogically pulling the louvered doors closed behind her as though that could somehow make him disappear. It never occurred to her that she was being paranoid as she crept soundlessly out the other door and into the sitting room to get a bottle of brandy. Her hands shook slightly as she threw open a cupboard and pulled out a snifter.

She couldn't cope with him when he was acting like this, she thought wildly. She'd known all along that his quiet, watchful distance was the only saving grace keeping her from being attracted to him. He wasn't quite human when he was acting like that. But acting like this, he was. Now he was smiling at her, kissing her, seducing rather than provoking . . . becoming human. Too human, and too male.

"Oh, God," she moaned softly, pouring the brandy and taking a deep, desperate swallow. He *was* so damnably male, so impossible to ignore. So compelling. So magnetic. She didn't want to think of him in those terms. If only he would go back to just watching her. If only—

"Where are your manners, Jenny Oliver?"

She gasped and whirled around. He stood behind her with that same rakish half smile on his lips. His shoulders looked massive in the narrow doorway. His shirt was open at the collar, as usual, and thick dark hair showed on his broad chest again. He was an unscrupulous, arrogant presence, darkly enchanting. Jenny swallowed hard against a sudden dryness in her throat.

"Manners?" she repeated.

He moved toward her with nonchalant grace, then reached past her for one of the cordial glasses sitting in the cupboard behind her. Jenny jumped slightly. His eyes held hers as he pried the brandy bottle out of her clenched hand. Her fingers tingled where he touched them.

"It's not polite to drink in front of your guests without offering them something. I thought you career women had more class and finesse than that. I hate to break it to you, but your style's slipping, Jenny Oliver."

"Uninvited guests tend to make me forget my etiquette," she countered tartly. "You weren't invited, so leave my brandy alone and take a hike."

Her voice was much harsher than she had intended it to be, but she was losing herself in him again. The drapes were drawn, and the room was so dark, so intimate. He stood close to her, close enough that she could feel the warmth of him and smell the musky, male hint of his after-shave. Her heart thundered in her ears as she took an uncertain step backward, putting some much needed space between them.

Gage reached out and took her arm, stopping her before she could move any farther away from him. Her skin seemed to burn with the contact and her blood roared until she thought she might actually faint. Memories of his kiss flashed at her suddenly, making her feel dizzy—the sweet, hard force of his mouth against hers, the oddly rough yet gentle touch of his palms on her face, his embrace, so frighteningly savage and strong. Even as her senses spun with the memories, his thumb traced an idle circle on her wrist. The sensation was rough and tender all at once. She bit her lip, struggling for the strength to remain immune to him.

The low, rusty timbre of his voice was her undoing.

"Why, Jenny? What's with all the haughty looks and the sarcasm? You get your hackles up every time I get near you."

She glanced up at him in panic. "A brilliant observation," she whispered unsteadily.

He shrugged but didn't release her. "I'm an observant man."

"No kidding." Her voice was painfully breathless. She tried to wrench away from him, but it was a ridiculously futile effort. His strong fingers held her fast.

A smile twitched at his lips. "Answer my question, and I'll let you go. Why do you get your hackles up whenever I get too close?"

She tried to pull away from him again—and failed again.

"Supposing I don't want to bargain?" she snapped defiantly. "Are you planning to stand here holding onto me all night?"

"As long as I have to. I'm stubborn as well as observant."

Suddenly, she was angry. Temper flared inside her quickly and brightly. With a sudden, sharp move, she managed to yank free of him. "Don't play games with me, damn it!" she snapped "We discussed all of this the other night at dinner, remember? I told you then that you allowed Timber House to disintegrate into a pile of firewood, and you try to provoke me every chance you get. If that's not reason enough to get my hackles up, I don't know what is." She paused to take a deep breath, fighting against the tremors of vulnerability in her voice.

He heard them anyway. "No, Jenny Oliver," he answered. "I don't buy it. There's more to it than that. You don't hate me. You're afraid of me, although I didn't realize that at first. I thought it was all men. It's not. It's me. I want to know why."

She tossed her hair over her shoulder and fixed him with a haughty stare. Then, suddenly, her anger crumbled. She pressed both hands over her eyes as her temper slid out of her on a tremulous sigh. "Damn you!" she whispered.

He was relentless. "Why?"

She dropped her hands to glare at him. "Because you're a man! Does that answer your question, Sigmund Freud?" she said gratingly. "You're both wrong and right. I don't trust you. And I'm not too keen on trusting men overall, either. They don't generally tend to be a very kind species."

Most especially with the women who care for them, she added silently. Then she turned away from him abruptly, already regretting her honesty, already dreading that another bridge had been built between them to span the gaps that she so needed. He was getting closer. He was circling in on her, drawing confidences out of her and tearing down her barriers. She shivered with the thought. Don't make me like you, she pleaded silently. Don't make me want you.

She felt his eyes boring into her back, then heard him turn away to pour himself more brandy. She couldn't help herself. She glanced over her shoulder at him. When he leaned back lazily against an old highboy, his smile was devilish and seductive again. Jenny's breath caught in her throat.

"White lace and satin," he said slowly, obviously satisfied that she had answered his question, and changed the subject. One corner of his mouth pulled upward in a grin.

"Satin? There's no satin," she said inanely, knowing immediately what he was talking about.

"An honest mistake. I didn't get much of a look."

"So take my word for it."

"Do you always wear such sexy lingerie beneath your clothes?"

Her hand shook as she brought her brandy to her lips. "I fail to see what business it is of yours," she snapped.

"Call it normal male curiosity. Was all of that hidden beneath that pristine little suit you had on the other night when I kissed you?"

Somehow she had never expected that he would mention that kiss. She had been *praying* that he wouldn't. As long as it wasn't spoken of, she could pretend that it hadn't happened. It had seemed like nothing more than an outrageous dream anyway—the Gage Pierce who had interrupted her staff meetings was the last person she ever would have expected to kiss her. But that man was gone, and this man had appeared, half tender, half teasing, and all too devastating.

"It's like unwrapping a Christmas present," he mused. "Keep peeling off layers, and you find the most amazing things underneath . . . and inside."

Jenny bit her lip hard against responding. The truth of the matter was that she always wore garters, and she always wore lace. It proved the small touch of femininity that kept her in touch with herself in a male-dominated and aggressive field. But she couldn't tell Gage Pierce that. This seductive stranger that he had turned into would have a field day with the news. She ducked her head in confusion.

Gage's laughter told her beyond any fraction of a doubt that he had read her silence correctly. "You really do something to me, Jenny Oliver," he murmured huskily when the last of his chuckles had died. "If I had been myself the other night, I doubt very seriously if I'd be in the position of having to ask you what you were wearing beneath your clothes."

"Well, then, thank God you weren't yourself."

The words were out before she had a chance to suppress them. Her voice was soft and honest; his eyes were suddenly candid. Understanding so fleeting that she wasn't sure it had really happened passed silently between them as their eyes held. For the brief time that it had existed, their agreement had been as tangible and as real as if they had spoken. The shock impact of the moment left her feeling stunned. Was there really such a thing as mental telepathy? Could people communicate without words, even when they didn't want to? Or was it just some people, who were very much alike, who were in tune with each other?

It didn't matter. No matter how it had happened, she understood. He didn't want to get involved with her any more than she wanted to get involved with him. He didn't want to feel drawn to her any more than she dared to feel drawn to him. There was lightning between them; it was hot, wild, and uncontrollable, and both of them were desperate to fight it.

"I think you should go," she added in an uneven voice. She shivered fiercely and bit down on her lip hard against the reaction. He was dangerous, so dangerous, and getting closer to her all the time.

"Drink your brandy and tell me whatever it is you came by to tell me, of course," she went on in a ragged whisper, "but then I think you should leave."

Gage drained his glass and set it down on a nearby table with such an abrupt clatter that she jumped slightly. "An excellent suggestion," he agreed. Then he demanded suddenly, "Do you still want my half of Timber House?"

She shot him a surprised look. "Of course."

"Then you've got it," he went on. "Raise the five hundred thousand I bought it for, and she's all yours. I've decided to sell out to you, after all."

Jenny's heart lurched oddly. So that was it. That was what was behind all of his odd, cryptic comments earlier. A strange mixture of relief and disappointment held her immobile for a moment.

He was going to sell out to her. All she had to do was raise the money and Timber House would be Oliver domain again. She wouldn't have to put up with Gage any longer, or cope with this disturbing new side of him. She wouldn't be seeing him at all.

"Why . . ." she began, then paused to clear her throat. Her voice was oddly strained. "What changed your mind?"

Gage stared at her silently for a moment. He was more than a little tempted to respond, "You did." But he didn't do it. Instead, he shook his head and stared broodingly through a crack in the drapes. "Priorities, I guess," he answered quietly. How much should he tell her? How much would she understand? More importantly, how much did he dare tighten the silken threads that were already binding them together with understanding and confidences?

Not at all. And yet he heard himself explaining anyway. "I got to thinking about them after we had dinner last week and you told me your story about going for all the marbles. I've had them—the marbles, that is—and I don't want them any longer." Don't want them? he scoffed silently. Or can't have them? He pushed on before he could give himself time to think about the difference.

"I moved to Little Beach five years ago for the express purpose of retiring," he explained with a small, almost self-conscious shrug. "I dreamed of leaky rowboats, coolers of beer, and days as long as summer. I was going to spend some time with my kids while they were still kids. Making the money to retire didn't give me . . . much time with them when they were younger," he added carefully. Then his words started coming faster, as though they were renegades with lives of their own. "I wanted to make up for that. I suppose I just want to get back to all those priorities instead of spending every day at Timber House, every day around you. You're deadly, Jenny Oliver. You make me think about things I don't want to think about anymore. You make me feel competitive again. You make me feel like trying again. You're making me forget my rowboats. You and your damned enthusiasm, your energy, your—"

He stopped suddenly, as though realizing that he was going off on a tangent that made him suddenly human and vulnerable.

"Like I told you," he went on, his voice a bit harder, "the money I gave Ed was an investment of emotions more than anything else. I just wanted to help him out. But Ed's gone now and I never had any burning desire to own half of an ancient hotel. Since there's no longer any emotion to invest in, I want out. Whatever you choose to think, I didn't enter into this thing to make six times my money, so I don't suppose it really matters that I won't."

He took a few steps toward the door before he turned back to her with the same strange, jaded smile that he had worn right after he had kissed her. "Truce, Jenny Oliver," he went on roughly. "You go your way and I'll go mine."

For a moment, she only stood there, the conflicting rushes of relief and disappointment so strong that she felt dizzy. Then she heard the front door slam, and the sound galvanized her into action. Clutching the folds of her robe together, she rushed to the door.

She was too late to stop him, although she wasn't even sure that she wanted to. As she reached the door, his sleek red Ferrari shot off down the street. By the time she was able to open the door, he had rounded the corner and had disappeared from sight.

She closed the door slowly, feeling strangely numb and disconnected. She walked absently back to the sitting room to retrieve her brandy, then sank down in a rocking chair.

Pieces of thought dropped into her mind like pebbles into a pond until the ensuing ripples were almost painfully chaotic. A Ferrari. Kids. That smile. His sudden agreement to sell out to her. None of it seemed to fit with the man who had been haunting and needling her for weeks. For that matter, none of it even fit together. She took a sip of brandy, her thoughts churning. He owned the ultimate in flashy sports cars, but he was a family man, obviously a devoted one. And yet, he had approached her today like a polished ladykiller—although with that simmering dark gaze, the term didn't do him justice.

Then, suddenly, her thoughts registered and froze. A family man—did that mean that he had a wife somewhere? He had mentioned something about regretting it when he had kissed her. Because he was married?

She groaned softly and drained her glass. So what if he had a wife? What did it matter to her? Wife, kids, or sports car—it wasn't important. He wasn't going to be her partner much longer. It didn't matter if he was a puzzle with a bunch of disjointed pieces that she couldn't put in place.

Pieces that she couldn't put together . . . yet.

6

It seemed only logical to assume that, with everything else she had on her mind that day in San Francisco, she would have forgotten about Gage Pierce. Instead, Jenny found herself constantly dwelling on the strange, unnerving side of him that she had witnessed the day before.

Ordinarily, the fact that she had so much to do in such a short period of time would have had her nerves wound tighter than a drum. Today, however, it hardly phased her. She moved through her chores absently, only half her mind dealing with the mechanics of closing down her apartment. The other half of her mind fretted with the puzzle of Gage Pierce and, in rare moments, remembered the disturbing flash of silent understanding that had passed between them the day before. The latter, however, was something that she tended to shy away from whenever it occurred to her. Even in memory, the moment had seemed so . . . well, intimate, she thought distractedly.

By the time she got back to Oregon on a late afternoon flight and opened the front door of the cottage, her nerves were vibrant with tension. The slow, befuddled way in which she had meandered through the day just wasn't normal for her. There were things that she hadn't accomplished—things she would have to make a return trip to do, and that irked her. And it was all because she hadn't really been thinking about what she'd been doing, she thought disgustedly. She hadn't kept and checked the lists of chores that were usually her weapons against days like this. Instead, she had been thinking about a man. A dangerous man. A man who could understand her silently. A man who was drawing closer and closer to her all the time. She closed her eyes and shuddered as she pulled her key out of the lock. That wasn't like her, either. Typically, no man could get close enough to her to communicate *verbally* for very long, much less in any other way. But Gage Pierce was different. He seemed to know where all the cracks in her armor were located. And he used that knowledge. Repeatedly.

She pushed him from her mind for what felt like the thousandth time, then peered inside warily to check on the whereabouts of Chesterfield before she stepped into the foyer. He'd ambushed her arrivals one time too many, and she refused to play the unsuspecting fool to his Samurai warrior, especiallly today. Then, when a few minutes passed and she couldn't spot him, she remembered that she had left him with Mrs. Arnold while she'd made her quick trip to San Francisco. Shrugging, she started to step inside, then glanced over at the old woman's house next door.

Mrs. Arnold. The only person left on God's green earth who could really get along with that damnable cat. A special woman, and a friend, one Jenny hadn't yet found time for since she'd returned to Little Beach. She'd dumped the cat on her yesterday, but hadn't delayed to chat with her. The thought stirred a fair amount of guilt inside her. She'd spent so many afternoons next door on the old woman's porch before she'd finally found the courage to tell Ed that she was leaving Little Beach all those years ago. It had been a time of tea and croissants sprinkled with cinnamon, and the old woman's tales of adventures in cities that Jenny had only been able to dream about then. Rosemary Arnold had married a shipping magnate, and although she and her husband had both been natives of Little Beach, they had traveled extensively. She loved the little town, but she had understood Jenny's need to leave it.

The memory brought Jenny a sudden and almost overwhelming craving for the old woman's companionship. She dumped the luggage she had collected in San Francisco on the foyer floor and hurried out the door again. A few minutes later, she was nervously cooing to Chesterfield. He was sprawled on the old woman's front step, effectively blocking her way to the porch.

It seemed like forever before the screen door creaked open and Rosemary Arnold toddled out onto the porch. She clutched in her gnarled hand what Jenny estimated to be the only object in the world that Chesterfield might be afraid of—a big straw broom. She batted the old tom on the rump with it.

"Get out of here, you lazy old monster," she reprimanded him. "Let the lady get by." She settled down in a rocker on the porch and glanced at Jenny. "So, how are you two getting along?"

Jenny scowled as Chesterfield lumbered away and she was able to curl up on the step, her legs folded beneath her and her back braced against the railing. "We're not," she admitted. "Not by any stretch of the imagination." She held up her scratched hands for Mrs. Arnold's inspection.

"Well, I'd be more than glad to take him off your hands," the old woman chuckled. "I suspect that Ed and I have been the only two people in his miserable life that he's ever had any respect for—and that's only because he knows we wouldn't hesitate to use the broom."

Three people, Jenny thought suddenly, remembering the previous afternoon. Ed, Rosemary, and Gage Pierce. Strange bedfellows, she thought wryly. Or maybe not so strange. They all seemed to play pivotal roles in her life.

She shook her head to dash the thought. "I'll keep him awhile longer," she responded to the old woman's offer. "I never give up without a fight. The broom, huh?"

"The biggest one you can find." The old woman paused, watching her intently. "So how did you find San Francisco?"

Jenny let out a loug sigh. "Chilly, damp . . . and wonderful."

"When are you going back?"

Jenny glanced up at her, startled. "For good? You know, I hadn't really thought about it. I've taken an indefinite leave of absence from Warwick Towers, and I guess I just figured that I'd stay here for as long as it takes."

"To rescue Timber House, or to decide if you want to move back here or not?" Mrs. Arnold asked bluntly. Jenny gave her another nakedly surprised look.

"I've never thought of moving back here," she answered quickly, too quickly. In truth, she hadn't thought of leaving, either. She hadn't thought of much lately other than Gage Pierce.

She shook her head emphatically as though she'd just woken up from a dream. "I can't stay here. God, I'd be out of my mind to give up my job with Warwick! No, I'll go back to San Francisco just as soon as I'm sure that Timber House can hold its own with just a staff of managers," she answered with the first thread of decisiveness she had displayed all day. "I can't—won't—leave until I've restored the inn and bought out Gage Pierce so that I know the place will stay in the family," she went on. Then she added more dismally, "Well, one down, one to go."

Mrs. Arnold lifted an eyebrow at her. "I know that Timber House is very nearly as rundown as when you arrived—although I have to congratulate you on that new landscaping. Therefore, you must be trying to tell me that Mr. Pierce has agreed to sell out to you."

Jenny nodded. "All I have to do is raise the money."

"Can you?"

"Probably. I'll have to talk to my bank in San Francisco, but there shouldn't be any problem. The president is an old friend of Ed's, and the land the hotel is sitting on seems to be worth a fortune. That's good collateral."

Mrs. Arnold nodded sagely and began rocking slowly in her chair. "When are you going to do that?" she asked.

Jenny looked up at her, startled. "Do what?"

"Talk to your bank." The old woman smiled innocently. "I assume that you'll have to fly back down there to do it. I'm just trying to ascertain when I'll next have to take care of Chesterfield."

Jenny felt herself coloring as she met the woman's knowing eyes. "It'll have to wait. Timber House can't spare me for another trip down there right away," she answered, and Mrs. Arnold only continued to smile.

"And, of course, you had no time to take care of it while you were there today."

Jenny grinned sheepishly. "I didn't have time to do much of anything today," she protested. Then she surprised herself by demanding, "What do you know about him?"

The old woman laughed richly. "Oh, Jenny. You're as transparent as glass. I hope you never change." Her chuckles rolled to a slow stop before she went on. "Well, Mr. Pierce seems to be very popular, despite the fact that he's a stranger—or outsider, if you will," she went on. "Is that the sort of thing you wanted to know?"

Jenny couldn't be sure if the woman was teasing her or not. If she was transparent, then Mrs. Arnold was incredibly shrewd. "It'll do," she answered.

"But you want more," the old woman guessed, grinning broadly. "Well, as I said, everyone seems to like him just fine. I doubt very seriously if this island's seen a party in five years that he hasn't been invited to. It might bear mentioning that he's also been present at the few that have gotten a little out of hand. But by the same token, he seems to be a good father. There were some initial reservations about him because he's so young to be ostensibly retired. But everyone loves a rich man, don't they? And Mr. Pierce is quite wealthy, from what I understand. I'm sure that had a great deal to do with the fact that people like your father finally accepted him. He made some generous donations toward the Little League field and what not—and not only monetary donations, I might add. I've heard tell that he put up that snack stand single-handedly. Of course, he'd got those two little boys, and both of them are active with the team. It wasn't an entirely altruistic gesture."

Jenny nodded slowly, feeling somewhat overwhelmed. The woman was giving her so much information so fast that she was having a hard time sorting through it. One tidbit, however, stuck in her mind—the news that he had two young sons.

"About his family," she interrupted quickly. "His kids . . . is he . . . does he—" She broke off, feeling slightly foolish.

"Does he have a wife?" Mrs. Arnold finished for her, smiling widely. "No, he's divorced, at least to the best of my knowledge. He's been living here for five years, and if he does have a wife, then he's been hiding her in the basement all this time. But considering that those little boys of his have to have a mother, there must be a Mrs. Pierce around somewhere. My hunch is that they've parted ways. No one really knows—it's probably the best-kept secret in Little Beach—but I don't believe that he's the type to socialize as much as he does if he's got a wife hidden somewhere."

"Socialize? You mean date?" Jenny interrupted abruptly before she could stop herself. The thought made her stomach knot oddly.

Mrs. Arnold chuckled. "That, too. But there's no one special in his life, my dear. I would have heard about *that.*" She sobered suddenly and gave Jenny a shrewd look. "Word has it that sparks have been flying between you and Mr. Pierce since the first day you set foot back on the island," she announced. "Seems to me that they've lit a fire in you. I can't say that I'm disappointed. I was always afraid you'd fall for someone who wasn't good enough for you, not alive and vital enough, if you will. But Mr. Pierce seems to be just the ticket."

Jenny stiffened. "A ticket to a dead end," she answered rigidly, swallowing hard. "I love you, Mrs. A., but you make a god-awful matchmaker."

"Do I, now?"

Jenny glanced up at her to find that the old woman's eyes were merry. "Yes, you do," she tried to respond firmly, but even she had to recognize that her voice quavered slightly. "Come on, you know me better than that. First of all, Gage Pierce has to be one of the most disturbing men I've ever met. And secondly, the last thing in the world I want to do is get romantically involved with someone from Little Beach. I have no intention of staying here any longer than I absolutely have to." She tried to ignore the fact that her voice lacked conviction.

"Ah, yes, the excitement and challenge of the city." The old woman's words were gently chastising.

Jenny looked at her sharply, feeling stung. "You always understood that!" she protested. "You were the *only* person who understood why I wanted to leave."

"And I still understand. Just allow me to act like a wise old woman for a moment. Age permits one to dispense advice whether it's been asked for or not." She shifted in her rocker and smiled at her softly. "Don't ever forget that the best of the excitement you crave so much can often be found right in your backyard, Jenny. I'm merely suggesting that you dig around a bit first before you make up your mind that there's nothing here. There's much more to life than city lights and fine restaurants. Take it from one who knows."

"That's not what you told me ten years ago," she reminded her indignantly.

"You heard what you wanted to hear ten years ago, Jenny. When you were nineteen, you heard me say that there's more to life than the security of a place where everyone knows your name. I'm saying precisely the same thing now. The best of our lives encompass a lot, both city lights and small-town comfort. And the wisest of us stakes a claim for both. A person's needs change as one gets older, Jenny. If you close your mind to that, then you're going to be in a bigger rut than Little Beach could ever hope to put you in." Suddenly, she stopped rocking and her expression became distant as she glanced over at Jenny's cottage. "You know, I half wish your father could hear this discussion. He got what he wanted, I suppose. But I still have to wonder if it's the best thing for you—or if it's the best thing for anyone to have her life meddled with to assuage someone else's guilt. How fair is it to take someone's choices away? We had a good many arguments about that one, let me tell you."

For a long moment, Jenny only stared at her. A small surge of apprehension tickled through her. Was she babbling? How old would she be now? Well into her nineties, Jenny answered herself. And the words she had just spoken sounded like nothing so much as a good dose of senility.

But Rosemary Arnold was about as senile as Jenny was. The crinkly blue eyes were still sharp and bright. She wasn't rambling. If anything, she probably just hadn't realized that she'd spoken aloud. Jenny fully intended to remind her.

"Pardon me," she said sharply, "but whose guilt, and who meddled?"

Mrs. Arnold's eyes swung back to her. "You never guessed, did you?"

Shrewd, yes, Jenny thought. Senile, no. She's breaking something to me gently. "If you're talking about the myths of Santa Claus and the Easter bunny, sure, I guessed. But something tells me you're not."

"No, I'm not." The old woman sighed.

"You're talking about Ed."

"I'm talking about sleeping dogs," Mrs. Arnold corrected her, "the kind that are usually best left lying."

"I never believed that. And neither do you. Come on, don't get secretive on me now."

Suddenly, the old woman grinned. "You always were a hard one to refuse." Then, just as abruptly, she sobered. "I always suspected that you'd figure it out for yourself someday. But you didn't. You still believe that you broke Ed's heart when you left here, don't you?"

Jenny shook her head slowly, thoughtfully. "I'm not sure Ed had a heart. Or at least I wasn't sure then. I guess I've just always assumed that he was angry at me for leaving more than anything else. He rarely wrote, never visited me." Old pain was beginning to twist inside her, and it made her voice harder. "I just found out the other night that he was undoubtedly lying when he told me he wasn't going to be in town every time I'd planned a visit up here."

Mrs. Arnold sighed. "Lying, no. Assuaging his guilt, perhaps. You never knew your mother, Jenny, but she was a wonderful, lively, exciting woman . . . much like you. Much too vital for this town. She loved Ed, but she wasn't wild about Little Beach. She wanted to move to Portland. Her family was there, she was raised there—Ed met her there, as a matter of fact, and brought her here. I don't believe that Ed ever really intended to take her back there—not to live, at any rate—but he told her so. I suppose that's where all his guilt came from. Of course, he never had the chance to live up to his promise anyway. Mary's kidneys failed when you were born, and she didn't even live to bring you home to the cottage, much less back to Portland."

Jenny's eyes narrowed suspiciously. "What's all this got to do with me?"

"Ed used you to pay his debt to Mary," she responded bluntly. Then, at the shocked look on Jenny's face, she softened. "Ah, Jenny, think about it. He didn't want you to stay here. He wanted you to have what Mary would have wanted for you—freedom from the confining small-town limits of Little Beach. Of course he wasn't going to let you manage Timber House. If you had, you would have made a success of it and you never would have left the island. And that's all he cared about—making sure you got out of here. That's why he never told you he had cancer. What would you have done with the news?"

Jenny fought off a deep, dark shiver. "I—I would have come home."

"Exactly. Ed Oliver was a lot of things, but he was no fool. If you ever came back here, it had to be your choice. No wonder he avoided seeing you over the course of these last few years. He had cancer, Jenny. You know what that does to a person. Makes them haggard, thin . . . the signs of it are unmistakable. You knew Ed as well as anyone did. If you had seen him like that, you would have known that something was wrong. And you would have come home. Because of him. He never would have allowed that."

Jenny nodded dully. Her emotions whirled. She didn't have to ask how Rosemary Arnold knew all of this. She didn't doubt that truth of it. The old woman knew everything.

That much she could accept. What she couldn't accept was the fact that the more time she spent here, the more all her old barriers were being attacked and torn down. By Ed's ghost. By Colby Barrett. Men she'd loved or thought she'd loved, and men who'd rejected her. Men who'd helped her build the walls around her heart, only to turn into different men she might not have needed barriers against. Shivers claimed her and she shook her head, feeling overwhelmed.

"But—but he left me Timber House," she whispered shakily, desperately.

Mrs. Arnold shocked her by chuckling. "Of course he did. If there was one thing Ed Oliver loved as much as he loved you and Mary, it was that damned old hotel. Who was he going to leave it to? A stranger who would sell to International Hospitality and have it torn down? As I said, my dear, your father was no fool. He knew you well enough to know that you'd fight tooth and nail to keep that place standing. I think he also suspected that you'd do it long distance. Since you hadn't moved back here in nearly ten years, I don't suppose he expected you to do it now." She broke off abruptly and snorted softly. "He took it away from you, then gave it back to you. He liked to play God, old Ed did. My question is: what are you going to do about it?" Her sharp eyes focused on Jenny again.

"Do about it?" she repeated weakly.

"Well, to my way of thinking, the ball's in your court now, my dear. You can stay here or you can go, but this time it's going to have to be your decision. No one's going to play you like a puppet anymore, my girl. And I suppose that's what Ed wanted all along—to give you enough choices so that you could make your own decisions. Orchestrated it well, didn't he? Even up to his choice of a partner," she finished, chuckling again.

Jenny gaped at her. "Ed wouldn't—he couldn't have—"

"Hand-picked Gage Pierce for optimum choice value?" the old woman finished for her. "No, I don't think so. But he probably wishes he had, wherever he is right now."

"Probably shaking hands with the devil," Jenny muttered darkly. Fury was slowly building in her as the shock of the old woman's news wore off.

"Not Ed Oliver. He was too smart and too stubborn to go anywhere he didn't want to go." Suddenly, the old woman stopped rocking again and pushed herself to her feet. "Think about it, Jenny. Make your own choice this time. But at least dig around in your backyard a bit first so you know what your choices are. And *that* is all I'm going to say on the subject, my dear. Perhaps I've already said too much." She reached the door, then glanced back at her. "Go home," she scolded her affectionately. "You've got more important things to be doing than listening to an old woman."

"Not when the old woman talks like you do." Jenny shook her head, feeling dazed by what she had told her.

"All I do is repeat gossip. And the problem with gossip is that it's always too secretive. The people who are being talked about should know what's going on."

"People have talked about this?" Jenny's response was quick, sharp. The old woman shook her head immediately.

"No, but Ed did. To me. So you see, I was really just repeating something I'd heard. Now go on. Go home and do something more interesting, something that has to do with today, not yesterday."

Jenny dredged up a smile for her. "Like mooning over Gage Pierce, you mean? Sorry, Mrs. A. It's not my style, and even if it were, I doubt very seriously if he's what's going to turn up in my backyard. *If,*" she added carefully, "I should decide I want to dig."

"Only because you're not in love with him yet. Give it time." With a last mischievous smile, she stepped through the front door and waved good-bye.

Jenny stared after her a moment, startled, then got irritably to her feet. She tried again to dismiss her words as just the ramblings of an old woman, but such an excuse was absurd, and she knew it. Mrs. Arnold might have been well into her nineties, but she didn't ramble. She was shrewder than most people half her age, and if Jenny needed any proof of that, she had only to consider the nagging thought that teased her brain as she walked back to the cottage.

If she hadn't been mooning over Gage Pierce for weeks, then she certainly hadn't given much thought to anything else. What was more, both she and Mrs. Arnold knew it. All the woman's talk about Ed, all of her revelations, had been designed with one reason in mind, and Jenny knew what it was. Before Jenny ran too far away from Gage Pierce, Rosemary Arnold was going to make damned sure that she'd thought about what she was doing first.

Unfortunately, Jenny thought, even Mrs. Arnold would have a hard time convincing Gage of the same thing. He wasn't running; he was armed and guarding the gates of his life. He might provoke her and play games with her, but he certainly had no intention of getting involved with her. And that, after all, turned the whole thing into a moot point. The thought stabbed at her in a way she wasn't sure she wanted to admit to herself.

Scowling, she paused on the porch, her hands on her hips as she looked back at her neighbor's house defiantly. Mrs. Arnold's intuitive wisdom could be damned, she decided. The bottom line was that she was a rational human being in control of her own life now. Wasn't that what Rosemary had been trying to tell her? No one was pulling the strings anymore—not Ed, and not Gage. No, she didn't *have* to dwell on Gage Pierce. She had only been doing so because she hadn't yet bothered to forbid herself the chance.

It was high time that she started forbidding, she decided. She reached around the door suddenly, grabbed her purse and keys from the foyer table, and turned on her heel again. She wouldn't be able to think of Gage—or anything else, for that matter—if she kept busy. And one of the best ways she knew to do that was to bury herself in pots and pans in the kitchen. Cooking never came easily to her, but she had a few specialties that tended to keep her up to her elbows in ingredients for hours. She would therefore go to the store and purchase those ingredients. If ever there was a time to whip up a gourmet dinner, she thought grimly, it was now. It was either that, or sit around and think about the conversation she had just had with Mrs. Arnold. And *that* would drive her crazy.

At first she couldn't believe it was him. It simply seemed too ironic and too outrageous that she should run into him just when she was trying to put him out of her mind. Yet even as she stared at his back incredulously, she knew that it was Gage. Although she didn't particularly want to admit it to herself, she was getting to the point where she'd know those broad shoulders anywhere. As he bent over the deli case, his muscles strained against the fabric of the blue polo shirt he wore. There was a ruggedness about him that seemed absurdly out of place in the supermarket. Before she even knew what she was doing, she found herself pushing her cart toward him. "Gage," she said simply.

His profile was sharp and strong. She'd never noticed that before. She almost missed it now, so taken aback was she by the way his shoulders stiffened suddenly at the sound of her voice and a muscle clenched in his jaw. He turned almost resignedly to face her.

"So who's playing ghost this time?" he greeted her, his voice as weary as she had once thought his eyes were.

She didn't know what she had expected his reaction to be, but this tired resignation didn't figure into any of her guesses. Her heart skipped oddly in her chest as she stared at him, searching for her voice. It had been there a minute ago.

"To quote the original master of haunting," she managed to say eventually, "I have every right to be here. This is a supermarket, for God's sake." She took a deep, shuddering breath, strangely depressed by his greeting. "Sorry I bothered you," she finished, turning and pushing her cart away from him. "Little Beach just isn't that big. It's nearly impossible not to run into people around here."

"So I'm learning. Somehow, it never seemed so obvious before."

She turned back at the sound of his voice and shot him a questioning look, but he only held up a package of hot dogs at her. "What's the difference between all beef and all meat? Damn it, they even have to make an ordeal out of hot dogs these days."

She couldn't suppress a small smile. "Take the beef. The 'meat' just means that all manner of other things are thrown in there as well. At least with the beef, you know what you're getting, although I'm still not convinced that they taste as good."

He glanced down at the package he was holding, his expression becoming vaguely alarmed. "Wait a minute. These things are supposed to expand or something when you cook them. That can't be good."

"Trust me. They're harmless."

"I think I'll take the others, even if I don't know what's in them. Whatever happened to those simple, greasy things that I used to get at the ballpark?"

"They're probably still at the ballpark." She frowned at him despite all of her good intentions to accept the blessing of a tension-free conversation with him. "You know, I'm getting the distinct impression that this is all new to you. I thought you were such a devoted family man, no after-hours staff meetings and all that? Is this the first time you've ventured into a supermarket?"

"Only on Sundays," he responded.

His voice was cryptic again and another small smile was playing with his lips. Jenny had the oddest impression that she was missing something. Regarding the hot dogs, or regarding her? She shook her head imperceptibly. It hardly seemed to matter. She must have been out of her mind to think that she could hold a normal conversation with him. He was always playing with her, always one up on her. She turned away from him again, feeling an irrational depth of disappointment.

His voice stopped her once more. "Those aren't hot dogs," he announced as though he had just made the discovery of the century.

"What aren't hot dogs?" she asked, looking back at him in exasperation.

"What you're buying there."

Jenny looked down into her cart, startled. "Not even close," she answered eventually, losing the battle to fight off an urge to laugh at the absurdity of the whole situation. Her cart was full with odds and ends designed to take her mind off him.

He came up beside her to take a closer look at her groceries, then glanced at her curiously as she chuckled. "That's a steak," he went on. "Top sirloin."

"Eureka!" she muttered. "You're right."

"And sour cream. What are you going to do with it?"

Forget about you. For a moment, she wondered if she had said

the words aloud. They had popped into her brain so instantaneously that she couldn't be sure. A thrill of panic flashed through
her, but then she looked at his unchanged expression and knew
that her words had only gotten as far as her brain.

"I'm going to make beef stroganoff," she declared.

"*You* are?" He glanced up at her with a look that was more
than simply skeptical. It was downright disbelieving.

"Well, Chesterfield can't do it. And outside of his charming
company, I live alone."

His next move was so sudden and abrupt that she jumped
instinctively. He turned on his heel and sent the hot dogs soaring
back into the deli case. "*This* I've got to see," he drawled.

Jenny watched him warily. "What do you have to see?" she
asked.

"You cooking."

"So drop by any night around eight."

The look he gave was long and level, as though he were
considering her invitation seriously. Her heart skipped a beat,
then started to flutter furiously.

"I've got a better proposition," he answered finally. She had
thought that he couldn't surprise her anymore, but he did. He
came back and reached for her shopping cart, then proceeded to
push it down the aisle.

"What in the hell do you think you're doing?" she called out to
him, astounded.

"Kidnapping your beef stroganoff." He wheeled the cart into
the check-out lane. "And watch your language. This is a G-rated
establishment."

"And robbery is illegal!" she shouted, catching up with him.
She grabbed his arm impulsively as he began to unload items
onto the counter, regretting it too late to stop herself. Gage went
still at her touch and glanced at her, his raven eyes devoid of
laughter and simmering now. Her knees turned suddenly to
water and she pulled her hand away again quickly, an odd little
gasp escaping from her.

"And temporary insanity is a great cop-out," he finally responded. His double meaning was obvious. A sudden memory

of their brief moment of silent understanding the day before made her head seem to swim. She knew instinctively that he was referring to it. Another hot shiver shot through her as she stared helplessly into his eyes.

"And I'm pleading it," he finished.

"I . . ." she began, then trailed off. She couldn't talk when he was looking at her that way.

He straightened abruptly, dropping the last of her groceries on the counter and reaching for his wallet. As soon as his eyes left her, she felt her breath escape her in a gusty sigh.

"There's no need to make a big deal out of this," he announced suddenly. Jenny wasn't sure if he was trying to convince himself or her. "Beef stroganoff just sounds a lot more tempting than hot dogs that explode," he went on.

"Expand," she corrected him automatically, still feeling dazed.

"Expand . . . explode. Same difference. It sounds dangerous and unappetizing. You were going to cook anyway, so do it at my house."

"Not for four, I wasn't," she reminded him, recovering slightly. "As I understand it, you've got two kids."

He paused to lift an eyebrow to her. Jenny felt herself flushing . . . again. "This is Little Beach, remember? There aren't any secrets here. Two boys," she recited. "They play baseball. You built the snack stand at the field."

Now both his eyebrows lifted. "Did you . . . uh . . . solicit this information?" His voice was oddly satisfied.

Yes. Oh, God, she couldn't admit to that. She tried to lighten her tone as she changed the subject. "You know, I'm surprised that no one's featured them in one of those starving-children advertisements. Are hot dogs the extent of your culinary talents? Why don't you learn to cook instead of hijacking innocent women in supermarkets?"

His smile returned, slowly and rakishly. "Because the women tend to be more fun," he answered. Then he asked abruptly, "Are you?"

"What?" she breathed. Oh, damn! She was losing control again.

"Fun. Do you know how to have fun, Jenny Oliver? Or are you all business? I think I'd like to find out."

Heat was starting to flow inside her again. Get it together, she commanded herself, then answered with a decidedly forced shrug. "Am I fun? Compared to what? The other women you've hijacked?" The thought brought something hollow to the pit of her stomach that she tried to ignore.

"Actually," he answered quietly, "this is my first attempt."

"It shows," she retorted, feeling inordinately pleased with his answer and unable to keep another grin from spreading on her lips. "You never finished letting me collect all the ingredients I need."

Even as she finished speaking, she realized that it was rapidly becoming too late to prevent the hijacking. Her heart lurched with a strange mixture of panic and anticipation as the bag boy volunteered to run back for a box of noodles. Even if she had wanted to, she doubted if she would have had time to protest before he returned and stuffed away the last of her groceries. And she wasn't sure she wanted to.

He handed them to Gage. There was something strangely warm and comforting about watching him carry them outside . . . like it must be to have someone there to zip your dress when you couldn't quite reach the zipper, or check on the pinging noise beneath the hood of your car, she thought. But she wasn't the sort of woman to lean on men. She had done fine without them for years—and she preferred it that way, didn't she? She watched him cross the parking lot with a sinking feeling.

What was he doing to her?

She pushed the question from her mind, both because she was afraid to answer it and because Gage was making off with her groceries. As she watched him, she realized that the only way she was going to get them away from him again was with the use of violent force. It seemed much easier to follow him across the parking lot.

He paused beside his car and glanced down at her. She couldn't read his expression in the murky glow cast by the overhead parking lights, but for that matter, she wasn't really sure she had to. She knew—sensed, really—that he was feeling the same thing she was feeling. Nervous. Frightened. Daring. She was going to have dinner with him . . . again. Even if she had a hunch that it was the worst thing she could possibly do for herself.

As though reading her mind, he began to justify the situation they found themselves in. "I have a housekeeper," he explained. His voice was rough. "She makes sure that my kids don't go through life with malnutrition. Unfortunately, she has Sundays off. The national budget isn't enough to get her to work seven days a week. Therefore, I'm left to my own devices on weekends. And you were right—I can't cook. I've found that hot dogs are my safest strategy." He broke off suddenly as though sensing the laughter that she barely held in check. "If you so much as giggle, I'm taking all this stuff back, kidnapping you, and forcing my chili dogs down your throat."

She bit her lip against her laughter and looked up at him with wide-eyed innocence. "Me? Giggle? Please. It's not my style."

"No?" He seemed to doubt that, but shrugged anyway. "At any rate, beef stroganoff sounds infinitely more appealing than my hot dogs. It makes sense, really. We ran into each other. It's convenient—my house is only a few blocks away—and it's fair. I'll buy if you cook."

Her laughter faded as she met his eyes. "Gage," she whispered, "I'm not arguing. You don't have to convince me."

Several weighted seconds passed before he answered. "Maybe I'm trying to convince myself."

She couldn't stand it. Full feet separated them, but suddenly, overwhelmingly, he felt too close. She shook her head nervously and reached desperately for humor again to break the mood. "I could try to wrestle my groceries away from you and spare you the decision," she suggested. Her voice trembled.

Her attempt at humor didn't work. His eyes held hers. "Do you want to?" he asked.

She cleared her throat nervously. "Not particularly. You're bigger than I am."

He nodded slowly, then turned back to his car. "It's the old white Victorian out on the bay." He said no more than that, but she knew it was as close to an admission as he would come. He wanted to have dinner with her. For Jenny, it was enough. It was more than enough. It was all she could handle.

She turned on her heel and started off toward her own car. "Lead the way, then," she called out. She didn't allow herself to think—she didn't dare. She climbed into her Mercedes and took off after him. It was a short drive, and she knew which house he meant. It was a quaint, rambling old place with just a hint of gingerbread, and it sat on the waterfront facing the mainland. The only disconcerting thing about it was that it didn't seem to suit him. A Ferrari, kids, a sense of humor, and Victorian charm, she thought crazily. His inconsistencies amazed her, and they were growing by the day. She was still shaking her head when she pulled into the driveway behind him and got out of her car.

He didn't speak as she followed him up onto the covered front porch, but when they reached the door, he turned to her abruptly and held the bag of groceries out to her.

"You'll have to hold this. I make the boys lock the front door when they're here alone, and they're under strict instructions not to open it for anyone. The only way I can get in is with the key."

She nodded and reached quickly for the bag. His voice was rough again. She was sure that he had begun to regret his invitation during the time it had taken him to drive home. It took her a moment to recover from the wealth of disappointment that gripped her at the realization.

"Where do you think you're living? New York?" she asked after a moment, fighting the sinking feeling in her stomach with sarcasm. She didn't catch the sharp, wary look he shot at her.

"We don't have bad guys here, Gage," she went on. "Nobody could be that stupid. What are they going to do—swim six miles to the mainland after they perpetrate their crime? The ferry doesn't run often enough to encourage murderers."

He didn't answer her, but only unlocked and pushed open the front door. Seconds after their footsteps sounded on the marble floor of the foyer, two little boys charged out of the family room.

They stopped dead in their tracks when they saw Jenny.

"Who're you?" The oldest boy spoke first, his voice an almost comical mixture of suspicion and amazement. So he didn't invite women over often, Jenny realized, and was shocked at the elation that surged up inside her. Out of the mouths of babes, she thought, fighting a smile.

"Her name's Jenny Oliver, and it's in your best interest to be very nice to her," Gage answered for her. He started down the hall toward the kitchen as he spoke. His voice was strange—rich and warm in a way she'd rarely heard it, and vaguely self-conscious.

"We're always nice," the younger boy protested, but his brother was obviously withholding a decision until he had all the facts. He took off down the hall after his father.

"Why?" he demanded.

Gage's voice floated back from the kitchen. "You know those Sunday night hot dogs that you're always complaining about? Well, Jenny is willing to rescue you from that fate. She says she'll make us beef stroganoff. I should warn you, though, that she's a little hotheaded—she even threw a glass at me once—so if you get on her wrong side, she's liable to get mad and leave. Then it'll be hot dogs again."

The boy returned thoughtfully to the foyer to give her an assessing look so much like Gage's that Jenny felt her heart turn over strangely. "Is that true?" he asked.

"What?" Jenny asked uncertainly. She was as flustered by his speculative frown as she was by his father's. Could it be that suddenly this little boy's opinion of her mattered more than she ever would have dreamed possible?

"Did you throw a glass at my dad?"

"I . . . uh . . ." Now, how did she answer that one? She cleared her throat cautiously. "Just once," she admitted.

"Did you hit him?"

"No . . ." she responded warily. "I was off by about six inches."

"I would have. I'm the pitcher for my Little League team. My coach says that I have a great arm. I wouldn't have missed."

Relief slid through Jenny so suddenly that it threw her off guard. She hadn't even realized that she was holding her breath, waiting for approval from this stern-faced little interrogator. She sighed and offered him a smile. "Well, feel free to give me a few pointers. Heaven knows, I need help."

He nodded as though giving this intense consideration. "I think so," he agreed finally. "Six inches is a lot."

The younger boy, clearly on the shy side, moved up carefully to join in the conversation. After giving Jenny an assessing look that was simply a younger version of his father's and his brother's, he announced, "I'm Danny. His name's Ben."

"Is this beef stuff going to take long?" Ben interrupted suddenly, clearly not as impressed with the opportunity to escape the fate of hot dogs as Gage was. "I'm starving."

"It should be ready in about an hour. But since we can't have Little Beach's prize pitcher wasting away to nothing, I'll start now." She moved off down the hallway. After a moment's hesitation, Danny hurried to catch up and skipped along beside her. Ben followed at a more dignified pace.

"What's beef str-str-?" Danny asked, glancing up at her as he struggled with the unfamiliar word.

"Stroganoff," Jenny supplied, shrugging out of her jacket and draping it over the back of one of the kitchen chairs. She watched Gage cautiously out of the corner of her eye as he unloaded the groceries. His hands looked so strong and capable. She remembered how they had felt against her face and wondered for the first time how they might feel against the rest of her flesh, wondered if she'd ever know, if he'd ever let her get close enough to know. The thought both shocked her and made something burn deep inside her.

"Beef stroganoff is a challenge," she answered in a strained voice, forcing herself to give her attention back to Danny and answer his question. "At least for me."

"*Now* you tell me," Gage muttered. She looked over to find that the wariness had finally lifted from his eyes, at least marginally. He was smiling again. Something hard and cold inside her—something that she hadn't even been particularly aware of—began to thaw slightly. His smile was only a small one, but it was a start. "Why did I doubt that you could cook?" he went on in mock resignation.

"Ah, Dad, come on," Ben broke in, clearly the logical one of the family. "It's gotta be better than your hot dogs. Hey, remember that time—"

"Doesn't that television show you like so much come on at seven o'clock?" Gage interrupted abruptly. Jenny glanced up at him, startled. He wasn't entirely joking. So he had an ego, too.

Ben looked perplexed for a minute. Then his eyes brightened. "Oh, yeah!" he exclaimed, then bounded off down the hallway.

Danny, however, remained silently at her side. Jenny glanced down at him with burgeoning interest. He's a brooder, she thought suddenly. The two boys were so different, yet they were each so much like their father. They simply reflected different sides of the man who had been tormenting her with his inconsistencies for weeks now.

"Brandy, isn't it?" Gage asked suddenly, interrupting her thoughts. Her eyes flew back to him.

"Pardon me?" she asked uncertainly.

"Don't you drink brandy?"

Had he forgotten since yesterday? she wondered, then knew suddenly that he hadn't. He simply didn't *want* to remember. She was sure of it.

She nodded at him carefully, and he turned on his heel and disappeared through a nearby doorway into the darkness of the dining room. "I'll get you a drink to help make the challenge easier," he called out over his shoulder.

There was still a vaguely raw edge in his voice. She had been right. He'd changed his mind. He didn't want her there, but his sense of social propriety obviously forbade him to throw her out. Either that, or he was struggling between common sense and common feeling. She closed her eyes briefly. She didn't want to know him well enough to know what he was thinking . . . but it seemed that she always did.

Her heart thudded sickly against her ribs as she turned to the cupboards and stooped down to look for the pots and pans she'd need. Then she glanced up, surprised, as she felt Danny tug tentatively on the hem of her sweater.

"Can I help?" he asked hesitantly.

A slow smile spread over her lips. She had one friend in this family, anyway, she thought. Just as she had begun to wonder if she had been out of her mind to come here, Danny managed to change her mind. His infuriating father aside, he was a cute kid.

"Sure. Just give me a minute to get organized, and then I'll figure out what jobs we should each have."

His shy smile broadened a bit with more confidence. Jenny was just grappling with the urge to hug him reassuringly when Gage set her brandy down on the counter over her head with a sharp click. She straightened quickly and picked the snifter up, taking a short sip. "Thanks," she murmured, reservation thick in her voice.

"Sure." He nodded at her curtly, then moved back to hover in the shadows of the dining room doorway. His gaze was the watchful stare of a hawk. Jenny swallowed hard and turned away from him to start making dinner, but she couldn't bring herself to forget that his stormy, simmering eyes were following her every movement again. She felt herself flush, and try as she might to concentrate on what she was doing, she failed miserably. If he was so perturbed by her presence, she wondered wildly, then why the hell didn't he just admit that he'd made a mistake and ask her to leave? She gave Danny a bowl of flour and beef to mix up with his hands, then turned back to his father, her sudden anger bright in her eyes.

"You changed your mind, didn't you?" she demanded bluntly. Her heart seemed to thunder as she waited for his answer. Standing there amid the intimate shadows of his kitchen, his son working companionably at her side, his response was suddenly excruciatingly important.

Gage drained his own drink and gave her a level look, not at all taken aback by her question. They shared another instant of perfect communication. He knew exactly what she was talking about.

"That's the problem," he answered quietly, "I don't think I did."

Suddenly, San Francisco seemed very far away.

7

What's the matter, Jenny Oliver? Is your courage failing you?"

His low, sultry voice was challenging. They were alone now; the boys had gone to bed. He was daring her to admit that she was afraid of him, of them. The fact both comforted and devastated Jenny. She hesitated in the door to the parlor and glanced back at him, feeling torn by indecision.

On one hand, there was an ironic security to be found in his taunt. It meant that she was dealing with the same old Gage; in that moment, he was as disturbing and provoking as ever. But he was also referring to that moment of unspoken understanding that had passed between them the day before. He knew that she was afraid to be alone with him, just as she knew that some part of him wanted to fight his attraction to her with every ounce of strength he possessed.

The proof of it was there in the steady gaze that held her captive. He didn't try to avoid her eyes, didn't try to conceal his feelings. His eyes never left her as he stood on the other side of the room and held the brandy bottle out to her in a wordless dare. Panic fluttered in Jenny's stomach.

She wrenched her eyes away from his and stared down into her empty brandy snifter. "I really should go," she stated again, unable to bring herself to look at him as she spoke. The clock on the mantel told her that it was very late. The shadowy parlor seemed intimate and romantic as the crimson play of light from the fireplace danced over the room. And a wary little voice in the back of her brain was pleading with her to leave.

Having dinner with him and his children was one thing. Being alone with him while firelight threw shadows across the rugged planes of his face, sipping his brandy late at night, that was something else entirely. Something dangerous. Something she'd never have the strength to defend herself against.

Gage nodded a little too thoughtfully at her response. "Yep. You should. The question is: Are you going to?" He approached her as he spoke. Jenny knew what he was going to do, but she didn't stop him. She only stared down at her glass like she were seeing it for the first time as he reached out and refilled it.

"At least finish your brandy."

"Why?" The question was impulsive, yet she wouldn't have stopped it even if she had had the chance. It had to be asked. It was insanity to test their control by dragging the evening out any longer, and they both knew it. Although they each had their own reasons, they had both agreed—albeit wordlessly—that it was best not to become any more involved with each other. And if she stayed any longer, it could happen. The memory of their kiss was almost tangible between them, obviously as clear in both of their minds as if it had happened the day before instead of a week ago. And it brought a sweet, dark sense of recklessness to the situation.

Gage raised an eyebrow at her. "Because we're fools?" he suggested by way of an answer, but she knew that his casual bravado was forced.

Jenny swallowed hard and moved back to the sofa. "And fools rush in where angels fear to tread," she answered softly, holding his eyes. "So what did you do with the brandy bottle?"

He didn't appear to be surprised at her response. She hadn't expected that he would be. The dangerous part about understanding him too well was that he could also understand her. And knowing that, she'd never doubted that he knew she wanted to stay. The realization had only surprised her.

"You know," she went on, praying that her voice sounded idly conversational as he brought the brandy to her, "you really shocked me when you kidnapped my groceries at the market. You're the last person in the world I'd ever expect a dinner invitation from—if that's what you'd call it."

He took the cue. He gave her a long, assessing look, then sat down as well. She noticed that he left a good deal of space between them.

"Of course it was an invitation. I bought dinner, didn't I?" he asked. His voice reached for nonchalance just as hers had, but there was an edge of understated humor in it, too. "Forgive me if I tell you that it wasn't one of the most relaxing evenings I've ever had," she responded dryly. Danny had dropped the noodles on the floor, Ben had thrown a tantrum at the thought of missing the end of his television show, and the broccoli had been done long before the stroganoff was finished.

Gage slanted her a sardonic look. "I never imagined that it would be the kind of evening you're used to," he returned. "As a matter of fact, I was a bit shocked when you agreed to come over. Didn't you expect madness and mayhem?"

There was something vaguely incredulous in his voice. Either he couldn't believe that she had accepted anyway, or he wondered if she had known that small boys spelled mayhem. Jenny looked at him wryly. "Of course I expected it. I knew you had two little boys. And some of my best friends have little boys. I'm used to their shenanigans and mishaps."

"But you accepted anyway."

"I'm here, aren't I?"

"Why?" The demand came so quickly that Jenny could only meet his eyes in surprise. "You could have been tearing up the dance floors in Longport City. Why did you come here to cook dinner for two kids and a single father who's voluntarily passed up board meetings for rowboats?"

For a moment, she was stunned by the oddly strained—and self-recriminating—tone in his voice. She found herself wanting to reach out and smooth away the lines that suddenly furrowed his forehead, but she didn't have the courage. It was all she could do to give him her honesty. "For the same reason you invited me?" she suggested eventually, softly.

He shook his head and polished off his brandy, then took a great deal of time and care to refill his glass. She noticed, however, that he relaxed slightly against the cushions after he replaced the bottle on the end table. He raked his long, strong fingers through his hair once, then draped his arm over the back of the sofa.

"Or for the same reason I bought the Ferrari," he mused, not looking at her.

She was startled. "I'm a Ferrari?"

He grinned at her. "You're not one for analogies?"

"Not when I'm the one being analogized."

"Well, I hate to break it to you, Jenny Oliver, but there's no better way to put it." Suddenly, he sobered. "You're sleek. Fast. Full of energy and power. My life-style is much better suited to a station wagon, but I can't resist you." The look he sent her out of the corner of his eye was oddly rueful. "I had to have the Ferrari," he finished. "What's your excuse?"

Her mouth turned suddenly dry. A very clear analogy, she thought, sipping at her brandy as something electric coursed down her spine. Her hands trembled slightly. She couldn't answer him.

"So what was this?" she countered instead, struggling to keep her voice neutral. "Some sort of a test drive? Let's see if Jenny will come play house, and if she does, then maybe she's not so inappropriate after all?"

Gage glanced at her enigmatically. "Maybe."

"Did I pass?" she snapped. Her voice was tight only because she knew that his answer mattered—and she didn't want it to. She detested the thought of needing Gage's approval. But she needed it, wanted it . . . and waited for it.

"I'd say so. You had those noodles up off the floor in no time."

Her temper tugged away from her at the lightness of his response. She felt as though he had robbed her of something by not answering seriously. "What did you expect me to do?" she demanded. "Walk on them? For that matter, where do you get off expecting *anything* of me? You've been doing that to me since the beginning."

Suddenly, his gaze turned sharp. He reached for the brandy again, although his glass was still half full. "Now you're the one playing psychiatrist." He paused. "I know," he admitted. "Defense mechanism, I suppose."

She was too startled and too confused to do anything more than take the issue and run with it. "You have more reasons for the things I do than *I* do," she accused. "But since we're sitting here chatting so nicely, let me use the opportunity to give you a bit of advice."

She was rewarded by a startled look in those unreadable eyes. "Advice?" he repeated cautiously.

"Yes, advice," she went on heatedly. "Give up. You won't succeed. You don't know me well enough to stereotype me. No one does. No one *ever* tried to."

His eyes grew suddenly hard again. "No one?" he asked, his voice edged with sarcasm. He got to his feet abruptly, downing almost the full glass of brandy. "I suppose that includes all those big-city lawyers like Colby Barrett whom you spend your time with?"

Jenny stared at him in amazement for a moment, then burst out laughing. Her anger disappeared as quickly as it had claimed her. "You've got to be kidding!" she exclaimed.

But his cold, obsidian eyes told her immediately that he wasn't. For some reason, he was genuinely angry. Like the last time they had discussed Colby.

"No, you're not, are you?" she answered herself. "But you ought to be. Big-city lawyers? Come on. Colby is probably the only lawyer Little Beach can boast, and that's only because he's crazy enough to keep offices in Brookings and commute all that way every day. And in case you haven't noticed, Little Beach is where I've spent the last month. I'd be hard pressed to hang out with lawyers, even if I tried. And I don't try—not even in San Francisco. I find them a stuffy, pompous lot." Her answer was smooth and flippant, and she knew she should have left it at that. But she couldn't. Something cracked inside her, something cold and hard and icy. She stared up at him as her gaze suddenly clouded with tears. It didn't matter that she rarely cried. She was on the verge of doing it now. Maybe it was the news that Mrs. Arnold had thrust upon her earlier, news that had turned all the tried-and-true rules of her life upside down. Maybe it was just exhaustion after two days spent scrambling to San Francisco and back.

Or maybe it was wanting something that she couldn't have. Even if she had dared to take it, Gage Pierce wouldn't dare to give it to her.

She heard her voice as though it belonged to someone else. "And I find the rest of the male race a hard, uncompromising lot!" she went on. "They take and take and take, and then they turn their backs on you, going on with the details of their lives as though you never existed. And then—*then* they wonder what they did to make you hate them. Well, let me tell you something so that you can at least judge me with facts! It's not just lawyers I don't hang out with—it's men I tend to stay away from. I've made it a specific point not to get too cozy with anyone ever since Colby Barrett took a powder on me and my father drove me to the airport and sent me to live in San Francisco with five hundred dollars in my pocket!"

His expression didn't lighten, but it changed. His broad shoulders stiffened and his jaw tensed, but he didn't look at her. "Do you want him back?" he asked suddenly, his voice as rough as sandpaper. "Is that why you're staying here? Is that why you had dinner with him last week?"

It took her a moment to understand that he was talking about Colby. She gaped at him, astounded. "No! Oh, God, no. Colby's still everything he was twelve years ago, all the things that made him turn his back on me to go get his law degree. The only difference is that those traits are more indelibly ingrained now. I had dinner with him because I had nothing better to do that night and because I thought . . . well, I thought it would be interesting." She paused, giving him a sharp look. "I didn't love him. I had a monumental crush on him. I was just too young and too desperate to know the difference."

He shot her an uncomprehending look. "Desperate?"

She stared at him a moment, then lifted her chin defiantly as she obviously made up her mind to explain. "You're the one who has me all figured out. You're the one who's dissected my feelings regarding men. Think about it, Einstein. He was the first male in my life to spend more than five minutes with me without constantly glancing down at his watch. I needed a lot more from Ed than five hundred dollars to start a new life. The hell of it was I never got it." She took another quick sip of her brandy.

Gage scowled suddenly and turned for the door. She could almost feel the tension simmering in him, although she was hard pressed to explain it. "Five hundred dollars," he repeated, muttering. "You know, I think this conversation will go better over Scotch," he announced curtly. "Excuse me."

Before she could respond, he left the room. Jenny stared after him in surprise for a moment, her heart pounding crazily. She wiped nervously at a stray tear on her cheek, then covered her eyes. More confidences. More secrets to share. Slowly, so slowly, she was opening the doors of her life to him, and she didn't even know why.

She jumped slightly when he returned, her eyes flying open again as she stared at him miserably. He dropped down next to her again, sliding his shoes off casually and crossing his legs on the cocktail table in front of them. He didn't look at her as he spoke. His voice was low and almost remote. Jenny had to lean closer to hear him. The faint, male hint of his after-shave made her think of how closely he had been standing to her the day before, how close he had been when he had kissed her, and her senses began to spin crazily. She told herself it was still panic that she was feeling, but she knew it wasn't.

"I was born and raised in New York," he announced abruptly.

Jenny blinked at him in confusion. "New York City?" she asked uncertainly, trying to figure out what he was getting at.

He gave her a long, wry look. "It's a night for confidences, isn't it? For explaining motivations? Why you're here and not dancing? Why I'm here and not in New York?" He scowled into his glass of Scotch, then went back to his original subject determinedly. "No, not New York City. Upstate. A little town like this one. I moved to Manhattan later, and when I decided that wanted out, I knew I had to find another nowhere little haven like that one."

"You can't go home again," she pointed out hesitantly, still not sure what he was talking about. "Especially when you try to recreate one town with another."

He cast her a irritated look. "Are you always so practical, Jenny Oliver?"

Only when I feel like I'm defending you against yourself, she answered silently, but she bit her lip against saying the words aloud. She had no real reason to believe that she was. It was just . . . intuition again.

"Were you happy there?" she asked instead. "In the town you grew up in, I mean."

"Happy?" he repeated thoughtfully. "No, I wouldn't call it that. Hungry, maybe. I wanted more than what my parents had, and I knew that I'd never find it in Billing's Lake. I always wanted to escape before I'd wake up one day and find out that I was old and had used up all my chances . . . and that I was still borrowing to pay the bills and saving money for a miserable vacation in the Catskills once every six years. At least that's what I thought it was at the time. I found out later it wasn't the money that I was hungry for so much as it was the excitement of making it in the first place. And by then, I'd watched it destroy too many people to enjoy the challenge anymore. My ex-wife. Damned near my kids. That's hard to ignore. So I retraced my steps."

His words were so abrupt and unexpected that Jenny froze with her brandy halfway to her lips. She looked over at him, stunned. For a moment, she felt absolutely nothing. Then panic began to clamor inside her.

Mrs. Arnold had said that details on Gage's wife were the best-kept secrets in Little Beach. He wouldn't—shouldn't—be talking about them.

But he was. And to her. Bridges weren't being built over their gaps anymore. They were being crossed.

She felt suddenly warm, and she ran her fingers along the inside of the collar of her blouse, trying to loosen it. "Your ex-wife?" she croaked softly.

"I didn't find Ben and Danny under toadstools."

"No," she murmured inanely. "I don't suppose you did."

"Their mother is still in Manhattan."

She gave him a wild look. "Really."

"She refused to come west with us to Oregon."

Jenny put her glass down on the cocktail table suddenly and sharply, a feeling of panic rising in her throat. "Why are you telling me this?" she demanded, unable to bear listening to the conversation any longer. She wasn't sure why she was so upset. Because the mention of the woman he had been married to evoked odd stirrings of jealousy in the pit of her stomach? Or because she knew that if he kept talking, he'd never be a stranger to her again?

"Because you asked," he answered gruffly. "And because I want you to know." His expression was grim, his voice flatly emotionless as he kept talking. "Her name was Abby. My secretary. Isn't that a kicker? I had just started out in real estate then, had investments scattered all over, and had finally decided that I needed a home base other than my kitchen. I rented an office and hired a secretary. Abby. Fresh off the train from Ohio. This was in Manhattan. I'd been living there a year or two by then, and I considered myself a native. I got a kick out of showing her the sights. She was wide-eyed and innocent and easy to impress. Or so I thought.

"She told me that she worked weekends at a nursery. That she loved kids. That all she really wanted was to get married and raise a family, and that she had left Ohio because she'd known every guy in town since they were all in cradles." He laughed deprecatingly. "I could identify with that. It sounded just like Billing's Lake. Anyway, I fell for it. I married her, and we had the kids. And then I found out it was all a sham."

He paused to take a mouthful of his Scotch, his eyes never leaving the fireplace in front of him. Jenny felt fresh shivers of intuition touch her skin with clammy, cold certainty. She was beginning to understand why he was telling her this. And his reasons weren't good. Her stomach felt sick.

"I'll spare you the gruesome details," he went on abruptly. "Suffice it to say that she turned out to be more of a whiz at investments than I was. And she had known it from the start. By then, Pierce Enterprises—the real estate end of things—was her baby. She took it over. I was too busy making more money, buying businesses, building them up, selling them again. Simple investments weren't enough of a challenge anymore. I left them to her. She got her broker's license. She had a good eye for that sort of thing, and did it well—so well, in fact, that she took the whole business in the divorce. Abby wasn't really out for a husband and kids, see. She was after those marbles you talked about. A foot in the door. That's what I was. An up-and-coming businessman who could teach her the ropes and set her up. I did that well enough, I guess.

"I might have just considered it a good lesson and left it at that if it hadn't been for the kids," he went on grimly. "But kids don't always take to the realities of an adult world so well. She didn't want custody, and, God help me, I didn't either. Oh, it wasn't a conscious feeling or decision. I love them. I just didn't know much about being a father. I was part of that generation who defined fatherhood as getting up in the morning, going to work, coming home, and kissing them good-night. I sort of automatically poured myself into recouping the business that I'd lost to Abby after she'd gone, and forgot I had kids. I was never home. I discovered the beauty of baby-sitters and housekeepers. Danny didn't agree with my assessment of them. He developed . . . problems. He's always been a quiet, sensitive kid, and those years played havoc with him. In short, I bustled him off to a family counselor and was told that he'd survive without a mother, but he wasn't going to make it without both a mother *and* father. My choice. I could give up the rat race, or I could ship my son off to the nearest home for disturbed children. I opted for Danny, even to the point of trying to save things with Abby. She was wiser than I was. When I gave her the choice of trying again and moving west with the kids and me or marrying the investment brokerage, she told me that she was much more suited for investments than motherhood. She stayed. After a few months of rowboats and Little League games and watching Danny get back to normal, I was glad."

Gage got to his feet again abruptly. For a long while—so long that Jenny began to think that he had finished—he only stood in front of the fireplace, staring down into it. The muscles across his shoulders flexed and relaxed as memories assaulted him. She knew without having to see his face that fury would be burning in his eyes. A small part of her heart went out to him, but for the most part, she was gripped by an odd, sinking desperation as she understood.

He thought she was just like Abby. And he hated Abby.

She stirred uneasily on the sofa. An aching sense of regret filled her as she saw herself through his eyes. She'd fled life in a small town and a father who Gage thought had needed her to pursue a career in San Francisco. And for nearly a month, she'd been obsessed with making money, if only to set Timber House on its feet again.

A fathomless sense of disappointment gripped her as she stared up at his back. It all made sense now. Understanding flooded in as everything fell into place. She could barely cope with the dawning realization that she had been harboring hopes of a relationship between them, but now, knowing that it was impossible, the truth seemed stark and plain. She'd been playing with the idea that eventually they would draw close enough to touch. She'd been wondering what would happen then. The answer was clear now—nothing.

She jumped to her feet suddenly, her emotions churning. The movement behind him was enough to make Gage finally turn around. His expression was distant at first, his eyes turbulent with memories of another time and place. Then he focused on her and smiled tightly.

"I'm leaving," she told him abruptly, her voice strained.

He looked startled. "Again?" he asked, a wry smile curving the edges of his mouth. "Shall I wage my assault with the brandy bottle once more, or are you serious this time?"

She stared at him, aghast that he could brush their conversation under the carpet so easily. It didn't occur to her that he had been living with the torment of wanting her for weeks, and that he was succumbing to it. She thought that he was being unconscionably callous.

"Don't," she breathed. "I don't want to stay anymore. The last thing either one of us needs is to get more involved with the other. I understand why now."

The look he gave her was one of weary resignation. "Do you?"

She didn't answer him. She was too desperate, "Gage. No. Let's just leave it at this and call it a night. We can't get tangled up with each other any more than we already have."

"Tangled up," Gage echoed. "I like that. It's appropriate. Sort of like falling into a net and then finding that you can't get out again."

"Stop it!" Her voice broke miserably.

His response was so sudden that she couldn't avoid it. He crossed to her quickly, then pulled her roughly, almost violently, against him. "Don't you think I would if I could?" he growled, the answer clear in the burning torment of his eyes. "You *don't* understand, Jenny Oliver. What I'm trying to tell you is that you make me want it all back again. The excitement, the challenge, the work. The risk of loving someone without being absolutely sure that the involvement won't tear my kids apart again. What happens if I let you into my life? Am I strong enough to watch you whiz off to the inn every day, knowing that I'm like a damned alcoholic, that I might not be able to sample even one little taste of the excitement of saving a business without losing myself in it again? Am I strong enough to pick up the pieces for Danny if he gets attached to you and you disappear? What happens if I fall in love with you, Jenny Oliver? *What?*"

Even if a response had been necessary, he didn't allow her time to make one. His mouth covered hers impulsively. The assault ripped her breath away. His kiss was at once sweet and savage, just as it had been before. And, as before, the same thunderbolt of electricity struck them as they touched. It was stronger than they were. She felt its power in the weakening of her knees and in the uncontrollable heat that swept through her.

She knew that she had to stop him. Anything that happened between them would only come to a dead end. Yet she couldn't find the strength to push him away. Her senses swam, making it impossible for her to speak, even if his mouth had stopped plundering hers long enough to allow her to. His proximity drugged her into acquiescence. The crush of his embrace, the smell of his musky, masculine after-shave, the taut muscles of his shoulders—all of it rendered her incapable of protest. Instead of pulling away, she pressed her mouth even more firmly to his, seeking his tongue with hers.

He broke away from her suddenly to bury his face in her hair. "You're a witch," he whispered, "so beautiful and so dangerous. I'm afraid of you, but I can't stop craving you."

His voice brought her violently back to reality. Her words, her thoughts, falling from his mouth. Jenny drew in her breath sharply and began struggling in his arms. "No," she whispered shakily. "This is crazy. This is wrong."

His response was quiet and resigned. "That hasn't stopped us yet," he murmured. And then his mouth was back on hers, brutal yet sweet, and any further protests died in her throat.

His embrace loosened only long enough for him to pull her hips demandingly against his. Jenny moaned softly deep in her throat, knowing that she was lost. She had every reason to stay away from him . . . and every reason to want him.

Gage seemed so lost in his own need and torment that she never really expected that he would hear the sound. But something of the surrender in her voice must have registered in his brain. His kiss became gentle and easy. She thought crazily of pines bending in the wind—their movements graceful, but the wind capable of bending them so strong and fierce. His kiss was like that, galvanized by something stronger than both of them, but infinitely soft and tender. Jenny moaned again and leaned into the strength of his body, returning his embrace.

Then, suddenly, he wrenched his mouth free of hers and stared at her, his eyes volatile with emotion. Even before he picked her up and carried her back to the sofa, she knew that they had reached the point of no return. And she knew that she didn't want to return—not now, not ever. There had always been something primitive between them, in their instantly volatile relationship and in their silent communication. Now it had transformed itself into the act of love. She felt driven to explore it, to see how far that communication could be pushed. As he dropped her on the sofa and came down on top of her, she knew that in some strange, bizarre way, they belonged together in this moment, if only for a short time.

She hadn't yet fully learned not to expect anything from him. She hadn't completely accepted the fact that he was impossibly inconsistent. Now, even as she expected that he would ravage her, he began to undress her gently. Her blouse whispered through the air on its way to the floor; her skirt fell softly on top of it. Gage's breath sounded shuddering and distant to her as his hands traced the outlines of her breasts, then pushed her camisole smoothly and easily over her shoulders.

When his hands came back to her naked flesh, fire exploded inside her. She tried to reach out and pull him down to her, but he resisted. He seemed intent now upon taking things slowly and reverently, upon bringing them together in a communion as pure and effortless as the understanding they sometimes shared.

She gave in to him, her only demand being to press her naked body against the hardness of his, then, in frustration, to work at the buckle of his belt until he, too, was undressed. With that accomplished, she was content simply to close her eyes, drowning in his touch. She shuddered as his hand found her breast again, closing over it as his fingers circled the hardening nipple. A moment later, she felt his breath hot and moist on her flesh. His lips closed on her breast and she arched instinctively against him.

The world melted into sensation. She pushed against him senselessly, aching with his touch. When he rose above her and parted her thighs, she could only look up at him and tremble under the impact of his burning gaze.

And then he was inside her, and wild, animal electricity jolted through her. That same communion, that same understanding that they had shared before, was there. It was shimmering and explosive now, but still as instinctive as anything else that had passed between them. Jenny met his thrusts with a small cry of disbelief, gripping him to her as the world and all its reality spun away.

He waited for her. She sensed it distantly, knowing intuitively that he was ready long before she was. Still, with the tender, sweet side of his nature that was so new to her, he held back. Even as she reached higher and higher, she could feel him slowing down to reach with her. When the heat finally exploded inside her, he held her to him possessively for a moment before release shuddered through his body as well.

It was a long time before she was able to open her eyes and meet his troubled, almost stunned gaze. And then, with a sense of helplessness, she understood. He knew it, too.

It wasn't just that they were all wrong for each other. They *were* each other.

8

Job, she was sure, had seen better weeks than the one she had just been through.

Its only saving grace was the fact that business was booming in a way that it hadn't in five years. The Fourth of July weekend had brought hordes of tourists from the mainland, all of them seeking the coast's lukewarm breezes as an escape from the farms, suburbs, and cities that they lived in. For the first time in ages, many of them had gone one step further than just spending the weekend in Longport City. They had taken the ferry across to the island. While Timber House still wasn't a study in perfection, the advertising campaign that Jenny had waged had at least brought its limited attributes to some people's attention.

Unfortunately, the influx of tourists had stunned a good many of the employees. The newer ones simply weren't accustomed to the demands of nearly two hundred fifty guests, and many of the older ones seemed to have lost their knack. During that holiday weekend, nearly all of them found it difficult to keep up the pace that so many tourists demanded. Jenny had necessarily been picking up the slack.

By two o'clock Sunday afternoon, she'd given up trying to count the number of hours she had spent at Timber House that weekend. Afternoons blended into evenings until it was all a blur. She just kept chasing around after the staff, trying to ensure that the holiday came off without a hitch. She never forgot that if their guests enjoyed this weekend, they would be back. If they came back, that meant more revenue, and more revenue meant more improvements. More improvements meant more townspeople using the facilities. With that in mind, she rolled up her shirt sleeves and waded into the chaos with grim intent, trying not to allow herself to think of anything else.

Like the fact that she hadn't seen or heard from Gage in over a week.

And that, if she was going to be honest with herself, was the other reason that the week had been such a nightmare of tension. Gage and his story about Abby were never far from her mind, and it didn't help matters that he hadn't called. He hadn't stopped by the inn or her house, either. It was as though Little Beach had swallowed him up. She hadn't even noticed the bright red Ferrari tearing around town lately. In short, ever since they had thrown down their gauntlets, ever since they had tried to convince themselves they were all wrong for each other and had failed, ever since they had made love, he'd disappeared into thin air. And she missed him more than she could stand.

Yet she couldn't bring herself to seek him out. What good would it do? she asked herself each time the temptation grew too strong and she found herself reaching for the telephone or driving toward the big white Victorian house on the waterfront. Any possibility for a relationship between them had been doomed from the start; she simply hadn't understood why until last week. Gage Pierce was a man with a will of iron. He wouldn't allow her to get to him. He was making sure that it didn't happen; he was staying away from her. He didn't trust himself, and without that, he couldn't—wouldn't—trust her. Because of that, the worst thing either one of them could do for themselves was risk a repeat of what had happened that night.

Besides, she didn't *want* to risk a repeat of what had happened between them. Did she? She had her own fears to cope with, her own ironclad rules. She had her memories of Ed and of Colby; she knew better than to trust. She knew better than to try to control something that couldn't be controlled. She knew better than to love. And she was absolutely terrified that that was exactly what she was beginning to do.

The buzz of activity around the hotel helped her keep her mind off it, if only because she didn't have time to dwell on how hollow and depressed she felt. It was easy to convince herself that Gage's continued absence was for the best if she was too busy to think much about it. Unfortunately, that state of affairs couldn't last forever. Her stamina was giving out. She'd worked until two in the morning the night before, and had been back in the kitchen at six to oversee preparations for a breakfast buffet. She hadn't even bothered to go home. Instead, she'd passed the short hours in between on the sofa in her office.

Now, however, her adrenaline was beginning to give out. As she stood at the sliding-glass doors and watched the tourists down on the beach below the cliff, aching weariness enfolded her like a warm blanket. With a long, exhausted sigh, she turned away from the glass.

Sooner or later, she was going to have to slow down and get some rest, even if it meant dwelling on Gage Pierce until sleep finally claimed her. She had a hunch that the latter wouldn't take all that long. Besides, her mind had been so cloudy and befuddled with fatigue the last few hours; she doubted very seriously if she could give *anything* any serious contemplation until she got some sleep.

The thought sealed the argument for her. With only a brief glance over her shoulder, she slipped out the door without telling anyone that she was leaving. The reason for her stealth was simple. If she informed anyone that she was going home, they would have a whole list of problems for her to take care of before she could leave. Nothing was so important that it couldn't wait until she returned.

By the time she reached the cottage, even Chesterfield's low growl didn't phase her as she trespassed on his porch. She gave him a haughty look of her own, then went inside to make herself a drink. As tired as she was, she still felt a need for some sort of artificial sedation. She wanted to pass into the world of the dead the minute her head hit the pillow—with no thoughts of Gage Pierce or what had happened between them last Sunday night, without wondering if or when she would see him again.

She poured herself a drink numbly and mechanically, then carried it back to the porch. Settling in a chair, she slid her shoes off and braced her feet against the railing with a tired sigh. After one sip of the brandy, she closed her eyes.

"All of Oregon seems to have come to Little Beach this weekend."

Jenny opened one eye reluctantly at the sound of Mrs. Arnold's voice and made a quick survey of the lawn. She located the old woman behind the fence that separated the two yards, a coffeepot in her hand.

"What you need is some coffee with that brandy," she announced, oblivious to—or ignoring—the fact that her presence wasn't entirely welcome. "All this newfangled nonsense about caffeine being bad for you is for the birds as far as I'm concerned," she went on. "I've been drinking it for nearly ninety years and I'm still here, aren't I? Come on, bring that glass over here. You look like you need all the energy you can get."

Jenny dragged herself to her feet and wandered over to the fence. "To tell you the truth, I just sneaked home for a little sleep," she hinted diplomatically. "I didn't get much last night. Or the night before either, for that matter." Or any night since last Sunday, if the truth be known, she chastised herself silently.

"Well, then, a little coffee isn't going to stop you from sleeping, is it?" the woman insisted. She topped off Jenny's glass with some of the strong, dark brew before she could protest. "From the looks of you, you'd sleep with ten cups of it in you. Besides, it'll give you a little extra charge when you wake up again."

Jenny took a sip of the brandy and coffee, admitting to herself that the old woman was probably right. All of the coffee beans in Colombia couldn't keep her awake much longer. She gave her neighbor a small smile of gratitude and started to turn away.

"Coping with a full house this weekend?"

Jenny paused long enough to glance back at her with a tired but triumphant smile. "Just about," she answered.

"Well, that's good news. Maybe you won't have to borrow so much money from that bank of yours after all, hmm? The one in San Francisco that you were going to talk to about buying Mr. Pierce out," she explained slyly. Jenny gave her a withering glance.

"Have you looked into that yet?" the old woman persisted with a look that said clearly that she already knew the answer.

"Borrowing the money to buy Gage out? No." She hesitated, trying to come up with an excuse that the woman might fall for. She wasn't up for another lecture—not with all of the latest developments between her and Gage.

"I've been too busy to get back down to California," Jenny answered eventually. "Besides, there's really no hurry now. I can live with a silent partner, and that's pretty much what he's been lately. It's having him constantly underfoot that I can't cope with, but he hasn't been to Timber House in weeks."

"He's just struggling with himself," Mrs. Arnold mused knowingly. "He'll be around again soon."

Jenny opened her mouth to protest as the woman's meaning finally registered in her weary brain. But before she could get a word out of her mouth, her telephone sounded through the open windows of the cottage. She turned on her heel again quickly.

"Oh, damn! How did they know I was coming home?" She started jogging back toward the house. "I'll catch you later, Mrs. A. Thanks for the coffee, but I've got to run. It must be someone at the hotel trying to find me."

"Maybe I'll see you at the Independence Day barbecue on the beach later," the woman called out after her.

"I doubt it. I gave most of the staff the night off so that they could go, and that means that I'll have to stand in for them!"

Mrs. Arnold shrugged. "We'll see."

Jenny grimaced and swung through the front door, then grabbed the telephone. Mrs. Arnold's damnable wisdom, she thought, was the last thing in the world she needed these days. She answered the phone with a gasp.

"Hello?"

"Running the marathon mile, or are you just in high gear from trying to turn Timber House into Warwick Towers overnight?"

Gage. Recognition of his voice came to her slowly as she struggled with disbelief. She stared blankly at the telephone, amazed and shaken, before her heart exploded into an erratic rhythm. Why now? she wondered wildly. He *must* have spent the week thinking the same thoughts that had been pounding at her. He had been thinking them long before he had let her in on them. So why was he calling her?

And why was she so glad he was?

"Running the marathon furlong is a little more like it," she managed to answer breathlessly. "I was only next door."

"Visiting the reticent Rosemary Arnold?"

His dry touches of humor still surprised her. She pulled the phone away from her ear and stared wordlessly at it again before a warmth that was frighteningly familiar now surged through her. She chuckled softly. "One and the same," she agreed.

"What's the latest gossip?"

"I . . . I don't know. I didn't have time to find out. You called." The strangest feeling of unreality wiped away her fatigue. It seemed absurd that she should be standing here and talking to him this way. Everything between them was too volatile, too simmering and dangerous to promote small talk.

But small talk seemed to be precisely what Gage intended to share with her. "I just wanted to find out about this barbecue that the town is throwing on the beach tonight," he answered conversationally.

"What about it?" Jenny asked warily.

"I suppose there'll be a lot of tourists there this year. Timber House is full for the weekend, isn't it?"

"Uh . . . not quite, but most of the guests have signed up for a seat on the bus, so you're right—they'll be there."

"The bus?"

"I managed to wrangle the bus away from the school district for the night. We're giving everyone a ride down to the beach for the occasion."

"Good idea." His response was slow, at once approving and thoughtful. "Free of charge?"

She felt her tension unravel at his tone. Business. They were just talking business. It was okay, nothing to get unnerved about. "The bus or the ride?" she asked.

"Both."

"Oh. Well, the ride is free. I'm not in a position to charge the guests for small touches. But it's okay. I enlisted my old third-grade teacher to go to bat for me with the superintendent, and he donated the bus for free. I have to pay for the gas— virtually nothing."

It was a long time before he answered. "Way to go, Jenny Oliver," he murmured, but there was an edge in his voice again, something slight and subtle, but enough to remind her that business wasn't really a safe topic of conversation after all. At least not in the respect that she could discuss her coups. She was vastly relieved when he changed the subject.

"Does *everyone* include you?" he asked abruptly.

Jenny blinked at the phone. "Pardon?"

"You said everyone at Timber House would have a ride to the beach for the occasion. Are you anyone?"

She caught herself grinning. "I like to think so. However, in this case, the answer's no. I can't go."

"Why not?"

Her heart stopped. It seemed like such an innocuous question, but she knew better. She knew *him* better than to assume that he had been wasting words for the last few minutes. He was getting at something; there was no doubt about it. She felt it. The invisible line of communication between them was never far off base.

"I've been left with my finger in the dike," she answered too quickly, her nerves tightening again. She realized too late that her voice had sounded harsh and cold. She regretted it immediately. Although she knew that Gage's continued distance was the safest circumstance between them by far, she still couldn't bring herself to invoke it deliberately.

She qualified her answer quickly, schooling her voice into softer tones. "I've thought about it, but I just can't bring myself to make the whole staff work tonight and have them miss it. After all, they've been going to this thing year after year, and I haven't.

So Timber House is running on a skeleton crew tonight while the bulk of the employees go to the barbecue, and that ensures that I have to be there. At Timber House, I mean. Not the barbecue," she finished nervously.

"You're not there now," he pointed out. "Who's got their finger in the dike at the moment?"

Her ragged sigh surprised even her. "God only knows. I sneaked away. As far as I know, no one even knows I'm gone."

There was a moment of silence before he answered. "The inn's been hopping. You're tired." It wasn't a question.

"Yes." She nodded dully. "Oh, God, Gage, it's been a nightmare. No one knows what in the hell they're doing—the employees, that is. It's mass chaos. I just keep chasing around after people, picking up the pieces. So far, there haven't been any disasters. All the guests are happy—except the Petersons, in room 112, who've had three meals delivered to them late by room service. I haven't slept, haven't—" She broke off suddenly, realizing that he probably didn't want to hear all this. But it was just so good to hear an understanding voice. "I finally had to get away for a bit," she finished. "Recuperate. Regenerate. Whatever. I'll go back."

"Recharged and ready for anything, no doubt. Well, go for it, Jenny Oliver. This could be the weekend that you single-handedly save Timber House."

His voice had abruptly regained its usual sardonic edge, but this time Jenny understood why. He would have given anything to be swinging through this weekend with her, shirt sleeves rolled up, black eyes intense. Anything, she thought, but Danny. She thought again of his analogy between himself and an alcoholic and swallowed hard, willing herself not to feel sorry for him. He would detest that.

"Maybe," she answered in a careful, neutral voice, but then something snapped inside her. Why should he make her feel guilty about her hard work? Before she could even think about holding her tongue, frustrated words exploded from her.

"Damn it, you're not missing anything! If you want to save Timber House, then go over there and guide it through the weekend yourself. I don't know how you feel about barbecues, but I would give my eye teeth to go! Why don't you drop the kids off here on your way to the hotel, and I'll take them!"

Stunned silence froze the telephone line. Shock ran through Jenny as she realized what she had said. She had never intended to meddle in his life, to tell him that she thought his motivations were unbalanced and unfair to himself. Not ever. She had wanted to sweep that whole conversation they had had under the carpet, to act according to its dictates but otherwise pretend that it had never happened. She squeezed her eyes shut miserably.

Gage seemed to recover long before she did, and his words shocked her even more than her own.

"Good," he answered. "I was hoping you'd say that. I'll pick you up in an hour. We're *all* going to the barbecue. If Ed could abandon Timber House on the Fourth of July, so can you."

He hung up before she was even able to think of a response, much less voice it. She spent a brief minute wrestling with her conscience on the issue, then sighed and dialed the number of the inn to tell the few remaining employees that she wouldn't be back. Then she dashed upstairs to shower and change.

It was just too easy to tell herself that he hadn't left her any choice.

He was late enough to make her wonder if he had changed his mind. Just when she decided that if he had, he would have called, her second thoughts made their appearance and clicked into gear.

She had no business doing this. Outside of her responsibility to the hotel, she had a responsibility to herself. Going to a barbecue with a man who had no intention of getting involved with her could *not* be construed as being kind to herself, she thought, especially—oh, God—when she was falling in love with him. She shouldn't try to change that man's mind when his reasons for staying away from her were carved in granite—at least in his own mind. She knew she couldn't change people. She'd tried twice and she'd failed both times. And she was terrified of trying again. She remembered how she'd struggled to prove to Ed that she was worthy of his time, worthy of the inn, and he'd sent her away. She remembered how she'd tried to cling to Colby, and he'd left her. She didn't want to try anymore. She didn't dare.

And yet, even as her pulse hammered in her throat and her palms grew sweaty with sudden panic, she couldn't bring herself to call Gage back and tell him that she wouldn't go to the barbecue. It had been so long, so very long, since she had done something just for the fun of it. She remembered his question about her capability to have a good time and squeezed her eyes shut. She hadn't been able to answer him, because she knew, deep down, that she *was* all business, and had been ever since she had set her mind to taking care of herself all those years ago. With a last shuddering breath, she turned away from the phone.

She peered nervously out the bay window just in time to see the Ferrari turn onto her street. Her heart lurched and she took a deep breath, trying to calm herself. It would be okay. There was safety in numbers. It was just a barbecue, and the whole town would be there. It was just . . . fun. Nothing binding. Nothing that could hurt her.

Could it?

She nearly jumped out of her skin when the doorbell chimed through the house. For a long moment, she only stared at the door. Then she squared her shoulders and moved doggedly to answer it.

"Hi," she announced nervously, throwing open the door.

Gage didn't return her greeting. Instead, he leaned slightly to the right, looking past her into the foyer. Jenny followed his gaze with a perplexed frown.

"What is it?"

"Where's the cat?"

She couldn't suppress a small smile. There was an odd comfort to be found in his question, as though Chesterfield was the only problem they had in the world. "The last time I saw him, he was asleep on top of the television in the sitting room," she answered. "Don't tell me you're afraid of him."

He cast her a withering look as he stepped past her into the foyer. "That surprises you?"

"Well . . . yes. I've heard rumors to the effect that Chesterfield shies away from *you* in terror." She paused, still smiling. Gage looked away from her, not willing to be reminded of the way her face could glow like that.

"Besides," she went on, "I saw you two together, remember? He was a regular pussycat in your lap."

Gage forced a scowl. "He was still in mourning then. Now that he's had time to recover, I figure it's safest to assume that he's back to being his nasty old self. This foyer has seen a lot of casualties. I don't intend to be one of them."

She closed the door, giving him a wide berth as she stepped around him to walk into the living room. Some of her tension was easing out of her, but she still didn't want to risk touching him.

"If he comes out of the sitting room, there's a broom in the kitchen that he might be afraid of. You can try holding him off with that," she teased. "I'll be right with you. Just give me a minute to get my purse and lock up."

"Get your purse and lock up?" There was a disbelieving echo in his voice that she didn't understand. She turned back to him uncertainly.

"Do you have a problem with that?"

"I don't know. I don't remember what your purse looks like. I do know, however, what everyone at this barbecue is going to look like, and it's not that." He pointed to her bluntly. "Do you spend your entire life in dresses, high heels, and designer clothes, Jenny Oliver?"

Jenny opened her mouth to protest, then clamped it shut again. The truth of the matter was that she had no idea what she was supposed to be protesting. She settled for backing up almost comically as he started to advance toward her, her eyes wary.

Then her back came in contact with the French doors in the dining room. She started to smile at the ridiculous picture they made, then sobered abruptly as he kept coming at her even though she couldn't retreat any farther.

"What are you up to?" she asked nervously.

Instead of answering her, he reached out and pulled on the lapel of her pink velour warm-up suit. "Who's this guy?" he asked. "Some master of the industry?"

"Who? What guy? What industry?" she asked, trying desperately to look down at her collar to see what he was talking about without having to scrunch up her face.

"The fashion industry. And Emilio Vasquente," he clarified. "That's the guy who's name is on your collar. See what I mean? Every time I see you, you're in designer clothes. Even your underwear looks like it came straight from Paris."

Jenny blanched. She didn't want to talk about that night. She didn't want to refer to it. She didn't want to remember how it was that he knew what sort of underwear she wore. She swallowed hard and met his eyes uncertainly as something inside her began to shake. He was grinning rakishly again.

"So?" she demanded. She tried to make her voice hard but it became increasingly breathless as he drew still closer to her. "I deal with the public. I've got to make a good impression."

"At a beach party where you grew up with half the people? Unless you spent your childhood in a million-dollar wardrobe, I think they've probably seen you at less than your career-girl best."

"I *like* to look my best, and it has nothing to do with my career!" she protested more heatedly this time.

"So do it in San Francisco," he answered. "Do it at Timber House. Do it here at home, for all I care. But don't do it at a beach barbecue—especially one where you're going to be seen with me." He paused to look down his nose at her in mock superiority. "I have higher standards than that."

She stared at him incredulously. "Are you crazy? This is one of my favorite—"

"Precisely," he interrupted her. "I rest my case. You're going to be the only person there—with the possible exception of the tourists, who don't know any better—who's wearing her favorite clothes. Everyone else is going to be wearing their grubbies. Grubbies, Jenny Oliver, as in old jeans that you don't mind getting sand in all the pockets of. Like this." He waved a hand at his own well-worn jeans, definitely a different pair from the well-pressed slacks that he had been wearing the first time she had seen him in the elevator.

"That's what people do when they have fun, Jenny Oliver," he went on, but his voice slipped a notch into seriousness now.

"Fun. As in not working. Something I've gotten exceedingly adept at. Trust me. I know these things."

Her eyes flew to his and she opened her mouth to retort, but the effort was ludicrously futile. He moved to brace a hand against the glass on either side of her shoulders and something inside her froze. The faint aura of his after-shave assailed her. The simple smell ignited inside her a thousand memories of last Sunday night, and for a moment that seemed to stretch into forever, she couldn't speak.

Then he reached out and yanked down the zipper of her jacket defiantly. Shock ambushed her as he held her eyes and that wide roguish grin touched his lips again. With it came her voice.

"What in the hell do you think you're doing?" she blurted out.

"*I'm* not doing anything," he drawled in the rusty growl that told her that his mind was made up and nothing would dissuade him from his opinion. "*You*, however, are going to change into something more appropriate. Come on, Jenny Oliver. You've got to own a pair of jeans. Everyone does."

"I—" she began, but then her voice caught in her throat as he pushed the jacket off her shoulders. With the touch of his fingers, another jolt of awareness struck her. She started to shiver.

And then, suddenly, she decided that she was going to have fun. He could tease her about her clothes all he wanted, but she wasn't going to let him get away with it. She pushed against his arm quickly and dodged beneath it, breaking away from him.

"Some bully you are," she teased, "letting a hundred-and-ten-pound female get away from you."

She hadn't really expected him to follow her. Somehow, she expected that he would share her same ironclad reservations about touching each other, about getting too close to each other. Instead, he chased after her and tackled her in the living room, his strong arms closing around her playfully and suddenly. As Jenny shrieked and tumbled down onto the sofa, she caught a glimpse of his eyes.

They weren't distant any longer. They gleamed with unguarded laughter. The shock of the sight almost made her forget that his full weight was atop her, that his body covered hers in a way that was both hungry and innocent. She might even have forgotten the hunger, but she couldn't ignore the innocence. It was her undoing.

If he had been blunt and direct the way he had been before, if he had simply tried to seduce her, she might have held strong against the assault of the yearning inside her. But he only lay on top of her, his arms pinning her shoulders, his eyes laughing down at her.

He cocked an eyebrow at her. "If you won't do it, I can always do it for you."

"What?" she breathed.

"Get you out of Emilio Vasquente's clothes and into your own."

She didn't know what made her say it. Maybe it was just the light in his eyes that made her reckless. Without missing a beat, she blurted out, "You're just looking for another excuse to get me out of my French underwear."

Full seconds passed before his eyes began to burn with a subtle passion just beneath the humor, and by then it was too late for her to summon her willpower against that look. "An outstandingly good idea," he agreed, but the amusement was fading from his eyes.

By the time his expression sobered completely, her control was gone. She felt the evidence of his need for her against her hip, saw the glimmer of promise in his eyes, and she swallowed convulsively, knowing that she was lost.

"No . . ." she murmured.

"I won't forgive myself easily for it either," he said too honestly. "But this last week's been hell. It's wearing down my resolve, Jenny Oliver. Knowing that you're so close, knowing that you're right here on this tiny island, I . . ." He trailed off, his lips brushing hers. "That's what I can't stop thinking of."

She had known he was going to kiss her, and she tried to steel herself against responding. If she could just regain her control for a moment, they might get out of this, she thought wildly. If she could be cool, she could disengage them from something that they'd both regret later. If she could just hold out against the flaming excitement that his touch created in her . . .

She couldn't. She knew it as soon as his mouth came down hard on hers again. His fingers found her nipple through the fabric of her light sweater. He played with it deliberately and the wall that she had struggled to maintain around her heart during the last week came tumbling down. She found herself returning his kiss with an urgency that seemed to come from someone else—someone without logic, without any self-preservation instincts.

It was her own hands that tugged her sweater over her head, and this time the act of undressing bore no resemblance to the soft, peaceful way that it had happened before. Their clothes fell over the floor and sofa haphazardly. It was as though they were hurrying away from the need to consider what they were doing, away from the need to stop.

When he entered her, the feeling of communion that came back to them again was charged and violent, not nearly as reverent as it had been before. They were two desperate souls craving sustenance in the one place they knew they could find it. She gripped his powerful shoulders and locked her legs around him, demanding as much from him as he could give. And she gave back as much as she got. She returned his every thrust with her own reckless need until release claimed them both and they fell back against the cushions, exhausted.

It was only afterward, as her breathing returned to a normal rhythm, that she was able, consciously and logically, to consider what had happened. They'd surrendered to themselves again, but the loving that had been so tender between them before had been wild and desperate this time. He'd been thoughtful before; tonight he'd been demanding and exciting. He was a prism of complexities. And she was so perilously close to falling in love with each and every one of them . . . if she hadn't already.

But she had. It was too late. The thought burned through her with nearly paralyzing intensity. Jenny gasped softly and twisted a bit to look at him, wondering wildly if he could read the revelation in her eyes—or worse, use that communication that they shared to sense it. Yet as she sought and found his eyes, she knew that that was the last thing she had to worry about. Even as she watched, a mask closed over Gage's features, the mask she was getting so used to by now. Protective, wary. He'd shut her out.

He sat up abruptly. She knew that the brief moment had been his time to grapple with his conscience—and his conscience had won again. The harder she tried to ignore the truth, the more it persisted.

Her throat closed and her stomach knotted. His voice reached her only distantly. "We should get going," he said, his voice succinct and careful.

"Should we? I don't know, maybe . . ." She trailed off, her voice breaking infinitesimally, then paused to get a grip on herself. She shook her head dully. She was better at rejection than this. She knew all the rules. She'd been playing by them all her life. And one of them dictated that they should still go to the barbecue. They couldn't give their actions any more recognition than they already had. They had to brush it all under the carpet and pretend that it had never happened. If they didn't, neither of them would be able to live with it. She pushed herself off the sofa and began to dress quickly. She kept her eyes systematically averted from his as he did the same.

"Jenny." His voice, tired and soft, stopped her as she began to pull on the warm-up suit. She finally glanced over at him, surprised. There was a tenderness in his tone that she wasn't sure she could stand. Not now. Not until she had time to put this behind her.

"Your jeans." He paused, then grinned. "If I remember correctly, that's what started all of this. The least you can do is wear them."

She nodded absently and turned toward the stairs, fighting the lump in her throat.

"Jenny."

He did it again. She whirled back to him, her eyes flaming. Don't do this to me, she pleaded silently. Aloud, she snapped, "Now what?"

He held her eyes evenly. She wanted to look away from the torment she found there but couldn't. As always, his gaze held her fast. "I'm sorry. I don't want to use you as a warrior in my own personal battles with myself, and yet I can't seem to help myself. I can't stay away from you."

She couldn't stand the look in his eyes. It made her voice, her response, harsh. Yet her only other choice was to try to defend him against himself again, and she knew he'd never stand for it.

"No problem," she answered. "I'm a survivor, remember?" She turned and ran up the stairs without waiting for his response, tears stinging her eyes.

She was composed, if fragile, by the time she returned. He stood by the door waiting for her. She watched silently as he locked up for her, fighting against the same feeling of security that came from having him taking care of small, male things. Not now, she warned herself. No more. She'd always stood on her own two feet. And she was going to keep doing it. As soon as she got through this barbecue.

Their conversation was quiet and strained as they drove to the beach. Just as she began to doubt if she could stand it anymore, he brought the Ferrari to a stop in front of a sloping dune that provided the easiest access down the cliff. It took a conscious effort, but she pushed her hurt into the deepest recesses of her soul as she got out of the car. She glanced around, taking in the huge crowds, the numerous barbecue pits, the families clustered on blankets, and she squared her shoulders.

Fun. She was going to have fun if it killed her.

The air was tangy, salty, and nippy, even in July. Her cheeks were rosy before they reached the first barbecue pit. Gage concentrated on commandeering two hot dogs for them from one of the vast tables and barbecue pits that the Chamber of Commerce had set up.

"Uh, this fun we're supposed to have," she began drily. "Just how does one go about it?"

He shot a grin in her direction but didn't meet her eyes. Unusual, she thought, as he responded, "Well, there's a volleyball game going on down there." He nodded toward the north end of the beach. Jenny squinted in that direction.

"They're jumping," she observed.

"Mmm." He handed her a hot dog. "Probably in an effort to at the ball to the other side of the net."

"They're chasing it all over the place."

"That's the idea."

She looked back at him. "I don't jump, Gage. At least, not on two and a half hours' sleep. Try something else."

He glanced out at the ocean. "Swimming?"

"I didn't bring a suit."

He gave her a comically lascivious look. "This alternative is sounding better all the time."

Something quick and sharp pierced her heart. Better, she thought, until afterward, until after you touch me and draw away. She steeled herself against a soft gasp and forced a smile.

"It can't be more than sixty degrees tonight," she argued, looking out at the handful of people who had been brave enough to take the plunge. "Only the very young or the very intoxicated could be foolish enough to go in that water. I'm not going in either."

He sighed dramatically. "You're being difficult."

"It wasn't my idea to have fun."

"How about some R and R?"

She lifted an eyebrow at him. "As in relaxation? As in something you can do with a hot dog in one hand, a beer in the other, and without moving? Now we're getting somewhere. Do you suppose we could find a warm place to do this?"

"There's a barbecue pit down the way that looks pretty vacant. And I've got a blanket in the car. Between the fire and that—"

"Sold," she interrupted him. "You go for the blanket, and I stake a claim for the barbecue pit."

She didn't wait for him to answer, but started off down the beach. Recoup. Reconnoiter, she told herself. You can get through this. It was just such hell to have him so close and yet so very far away.

She took a deep breath, trying not to think about it, as she dropped down beside the fire. She helped herself to another hot dog from a nearby picnic table, speared it, and held it out over the flames. With her other hand, she dug into the cooler beside the table for a beer. She huddled closer to the fire, trying to keep her mind blank as she glanced around at the crowd.

And then she saw Danny.

She stared at him for a moment, not quite understanding. He played in the sand far up the beach, clutching a hamburger in one hand as he patted a sand castle into perfection with the other. Ben stood behind him, watching the proceedings with a look that said clearly that he thought such activities were for children—and that he wished he could bring himself to behave like a child. A stocky, elderly woman stood beside them. Jenny sat up straighter as comprehension jolted through her.

The boys' absence had been nagging at the back of her brain since Gage had picked her up. He had said that they were all going to the barbecue, yet he had arrived alone. But so much had happened so fast that she'd never had the opportunity to ask him about it.

She whirled around in the sand to face him as she heard his footsteps behind her. "Your kids . . ." she began, her voice tight.

"What about them?" he asked. He dropped the blanket beside her, then turned back to the picnic table and lifted the bun off his hot dog to squirt more mustard on it.

"They're here."

"Of course they're here." He sank down beside her and gave her an odd look. "Where'd you expect them to be? The entire population of the island is here."

"You sent them with your housekeeper," she pushed on, suddenly beyond caring that her voice was growing strident.

He held her gaze. "Yes." She had known that it wouldn't be long before he picked up on her train of thought. It was just that she'd been hoping, praying, that he would say something to make her feel foolish for thinking what she was thinking. But the look in his eyes told her that he wouldn't.

She closed her eyes briefly, then forced herself to look at him again. "Because you wanted to keep them away from me?" she guessed, reading the answer in his eyes.

He scowled darkly and reached into the cooler for a beer. "That's putting it a little dramatically, don't you think?" His voice grew gradually rougher.

She swallowed hard to force down a piece of hot dog that felt like a wad of sandpaper in her throat. "I don't know. You tell me."

He shot her a deliberately enigmatic glance. "Tell you what?"

"Did you send them with your housekeeper because you don't want to tangle them up in this weakness you have for me?" she demanded, her voice growing louder as she felt herself losing her tenuous grip on her self-control. "Or just because you were hoping for a quickie before we left? That's the only reason we're here together tonight, isn't it? The only reason you made love with me, the only reason you keep seeing me! Because you're thinking you can keep me in a nice little outside compartment of your life, away from your kids, in a place where I can't upset the delicate balance of things! If you thought there was any chance you could fall in love with me, you wouldn't risk it by continuing to spend time with me. You'd be in Alaska by now!" Her voice kept rising in anguish and fury.

His expression was grim, tired, almost haggard. It hurt more than anything had yet. "What do you want me to say? Do you want me to deny it? I can't, and we both know why. I'm not going to risk the emotional well-being of my children on you. They don't need—I don't need—to start loving another woman only to have her turn around and leave us when Timber House is all fixed up. I won't let them start getting attached to someone I'm not completely sure of. It's not so complex, really. I'm just protecting my children."

"Your children?" she shot back. "Or the coward you are at heart?"

He flinched. For a brief second, a horrible, aching regret claimed her. She didn't want to hurt him. But the hurt inside her own heart was too much, too heavy, for her to be able to cope with anything else.

"Jenny," he ground out eventually, "you're not being fair."

"Not being fair?" she whispered incredulously, her voice raw. "And you are?"

Suddenly, he was angry. The eyes he turned on her were chips of glass, cold and forbidding. She didn't see the torment in them. She only saw the fury.

He gripped her shoulder and pulled her roughly, almost violently, around to face him as she stared out at the ocean, trying to get control of herself. She tried not to think about the

148

way that same iron grip could be so tender. Her heart in her throat, she stared at him.

"You want me to be fair?" he demanded. "Okay. I'll be fair if you'll be honest. Tell me, Jenny Oliver . . . tell me just what is it you're planning to do when Timber House has been restored. Are you going back to San Francisco?"

She wasn't prepared for the question. And it wasn't one she knew how to answer. In the small space of time it took her to blink at him miserably, he went on.

"That's about what I thought," he finished grimly. "And you wonder why I sent my kids here with my housekeeper. You're all Danny's been talking about all week. Your beef stuff —his words, not mine. Your clutziness. He's still blaming you for spilling the noodles. He says you bumped into him when the water for the broccoli boiled over." Suddenly, his voice became intense again. "I won't do it, Jenny. I won't let him start loving you."

"Of course not. First you've got to let yourself!"

She didn't wait for a response. She didn't really want one. She'd had all that she could handle. Her temples throbbed with a raw, primitive hurt as she scrambled to her feet.

But his voice made her pause again, if only because it was suddenly more weary than hard. "I'm not sure I've got a hell of a lot of choice on that score," he murmured grimly.

Her heart lurched strangely, yearningly, but only once. She wouldn't allow herself more than that one fleeting spasm of hope. Hope destroyed you, clouded your mind to reality. She wouldn't entertain it ever again.

She whirled on her heel to face him again. "We always have choices, Gage," she bit out. "And no one can take us anywhere we don't want to go. I'm not your problem. I'm not enticing you back into the business world. You *belong* there. A big part of you still wants to be there. And I'm not so much of a gypsy that you have to worry about me stealing Danny's heart—or yours—and then disappearing. I lived in one place for twenty years, and another for the last nine—not exactly your average traveling show! Maybe you ought to stop trying to fit yourself into retirement like a square peg into a round hole! Maybe you ought to stop worrying about where I'm going and worry about where

you want me to be! Maybe you ought to stop being a coward an—
just let me love you!"

It took her all of two seconds to realize what she had sai—
seconds when her breath came hard and fast and their eyes hel—
And then she didn't dare wait for his reaction. She turned on h—
heel and ran.

The hell of it was, she was a coward, too.

9

Jage Pierce is on line one. Do you want to take it here at the
sk, or shall I tell him to hold on until you can get up to your
fice?"

Jenny's heart did an uncomfortable little flip-flop. The lobby
emed to shade to black so quickly that she wondered crazily if
e were going to faint. She had known that it would have to
ppen sooner or later. She'd known that he'd call. She just
ought that she'd have more time. She wasn't sure she was
ady for him yet.

Her knuckles whitened slightly as she gripped the edge of the
gistration desk for support. "Gage?" she repeated dazedly, her
e one of quick, panicked thought.

The clerk looked at her strangely. "That's right. On line one,"
repeated uncertainly. "Do you—"

"I'll take it in Horace's office," she interrupted him abruptly,
llecting herself. She stepped into the room behind the desk and
sed the door. It was blessedly vacant. She sank weakly against
door as she stared at the blinking button on the telephone as
ugh it were a poisonous snake.

Gage. On line one. The thoughts hurtled through her brai
only to be topped off by the clincher: *Now. If you're going to c
this, it's got to be now.*

She'd seen him only occasionally in the three weeks that ha
passed since the Fourth of July. They'd been distant and poli
with each other every time. And every time, Jenny had becon
more and more painfully sure of a startling truth: she loved Gag
She loved the way he smiled, and she loved the way he frowne
She loved him when he was unyielding, and she loved the so
spot in him that would have him donate five hundred thousai
dollars to an old man. And, for the third time in her life, for t
most important time in her life, she was going to have to risk h
heart and make a grandstand play for him if she was going
have him.

When she'd realized that, she'd hatched her plan.

It was simple, really, although it involved a bit of deceit. S
was going to convince him that he needed to stay active with t
inn if he was going to save his five-hundred-thousand-dol
investment. She was going to convince him that he'd rather
back to work than sit by impotently while his money went do
the drain. And she was going to prove to him that the love
gave Danny was more important than all the hours he spent w
him. She even knew how she was going to go about it. She w
simply scared.

It wasn't the kind of fear that had haunted her throughout I
life. In the long, empty nights that had passed since the Fourth
July, she'd finally come to terms with what her return to Li
Beach had done to her. It had robbed her of her failures. S
knew now that she hadn't really failed with Ed. She just had
known that she had won; he'd never let her know. And :
hadn't really failed with Colby because winning was for kee
and she hadn't wanted him for keeps.

No, she was frightened for another reason. She was frighter
because she wasn't trying to prove *herself* to Gage Pierce. S
was going to try to prove himself to him, which was a m
harder battle, and one in which failure would be unthinka
She loved him. She refused to lose him. She couldn't let him
and she couldn't go on the way they were.

She stared at the telephone, unconsciously squaring her shoulders. He'd be calling because he wanted his money, she thought. Eight weeks had passed since he had first told her that he would sell out to her. He'd be losing patience with her right about now, and that was undoubtedly the reason he was calling. So she couldn't stall anymore. She couldn't gather her courage anymore. If the hotel and his money were going to be her chief weapons in this war, then she'd have to launch the attack now.

She sat down hard in Horace's chair and ran nervous fingers through her hair. The button on the telephone kept blinking at her. She swallowed drily and reached for the receiver.

"Yes?" Her greeting lacked the propriety that their previous meetings had boasted, but it was the best she could do under the circumstances.

Gage's voice came back to her as oddly intimate as ever. Jenny fought against a shiver but fell miserably short of triumphing over it. "Ah, I was right," he answered. "Although I was just beginning to wonder. It took you long enough to answer the phone."

Another cryptic Pierce comment. "I'm not the least bit interested in playing games with you, Gage," she responded, her voice tight. "What's more, I don't have the time. This place is a madhouse. What were you right about, and what do you want?" Good, she thought. Just the right touch of irritability and exhaustion.

"Cranky today, aren't you?" It had been so long since she'd heard that gleefully taunting voice that it very nearly had a debilitating effect on her.

"You'd be cranky, too, if half your staff was out with the flu and you were trying to catch up on a lot of back work," she grumbled.

"So life goes on at Timber House," he drawled. So far, there wasn't the slightest edge in his voice. He actually sounded cheerful. She frowned. "History might be in the making on Bayshore Drive," he went on, "but you'd never know it over at the inn. Jenny Oliver has her shirt sleeves rolled up, and the show will go on."

"What in the hell are you talking about?" she demanded.

"Gage, really, I don't have time to play guessing games with you. The decorator will be here in half an hour."

"Decorator?" He sounded startled.

"Kevin Washman from Sacramento," she supplied. "Have you heard of him? I was lucky to get him. Ever since he did those rooms for Warwick Towers and for those places in Beverly Hills, he's been in high demand. Luckily, I got to know him when he did the Warwick, and he agreed to fly up here to see what he could do."

There was a long pause. "Washman? Expensive, isn't he?"

"Worth it," she corrected him.

"What are you having him do?"

"The east wing."

"The *entire* east wing? There must be twenty-five rooms over there."

Jenny smiled to herself. "Twenty-seven. Anyway, what was it you were talking about?"

Another pause, longer this time. He was thinking. And, with any luck, he was thinking about the astronomical bill Kevin Washman would have presented her with—if he had been coming. She bit back a laugh and waited. This wasn't as difficult as she'd thought.

"That's exactly what I was trying to tell you before you got off on decorators," he replied in the rough voice she was coming to know so well. "You asked me what I was right about and what I wanted, and I was answering you."

"You couldn't prove it by me," she muttered.

He ignored her gibe with the dauntless perseverance that she was actually coming to enjoy. "I was right when I guessed that you were at Timber House because I didn't get an answer when I called your house. And I'm calling because history is in the making," he answered with mock patience.

"You don't say," she responded sarcastically. "Don't tell me—your smile is making its annual appearance tonight at eight. Is that the history you're talking about?"

"Charming disposition you have today," he commented without answering her question.

"You bring out the best in me."

"I try."

"Are we going to sit here prodding each other all afternoon, or can I go back to work now? As I said, Kevin Washman—"

"Forget Kevin Washman. Mankind is taking a giant step forward within the hour."

"And what might that be?" she asked, curious in spite of herself, then realized that he had given her a perfect opening. "I suppose it's too much to hope that you're going to the moon? That *would* be a giant step forward for mankind, come to think of it. The first mule in space," she mused.

"Mule?" he asked with infuriating calm.

"It was the first thing I could think of that's stubborn and cowardly."

"You *are* on a roll today, aren't you?"

You don't know the half of it, she thought with grim intent, but schooled her voice into a quarrelsome, flippant tone. "As I remember it, I still owe you a few. We left the score a little unbalanced on the Fourth of July."

Silence filled the line suddenly, and tension began to build as it continued. She'd finally gotten to him, then.

"So if you're not going to the moon, what *are* you up to?" she asked after a moment, her voice somewhat softer. "What kind of history are you making?"

For a moment, she had to wonder if he was going to answer her or just hang up. Then there was the other possibility—that he would give as good as he got and come back at her with a few well-aimed jabs all his own. That would have been preferable. Anything to get him riled up, to crack through that stubborn resolve. Jenny found herself holding her breath as she waited for him to say or do something.

But he only chuckled shortly. "The culinary kind," he answered. She sensed that he was, for some reason, determined to be on his best behavior tonight. "That crack you once made about my kids and the starving-children campaigns has inspired me to new gourmet heights. I'm going to do the Sunday night hot dogs on the barbecue grill this time. This could be something you really wouldn't want to miss."

Jenny caught her breath. There was an undercurrent of

surrender in his voice. So soon? But then, surrendering to her and surrendering to himself were two completely different things. The only way she was going to win Gage Pierce was to have him do both. This, however, was a start.

"Are you inviting me to dinner?" she asked softly.

"You got it," he answered with that same vaguely resigned tone. "And you don't even have to cook this time. What's more, I take full responsibility for all spillages."

"Now, *that's* saying something," she drawled, stalling for time. He *was* inviting her to dinner. Now what? He should have been demanding his money back. He should have been speaking with cool, remote propriety, the way he had done every time she had seen him all month, the way that had both torn her heart out and had provided her with the courage she needed to face the fact that she loved him and was going to fight for him. But the bulk of her plot had been based on the business, and now he was throwing her a curve. Well, she could launch a personal attack, too. Actually, she thought, the two might fit together nicely.

"That's not," he answered, breaking into her thoughts.

"What's not?" she asked smoothly, her thoughts still churning.

"Your answer—it didn't say anything at all. I was looking more for a yes or a no, as in, 'Yes, I'll come to dinner,' or, 'No, I won't.'"

"This from a man who holds the world's record for cryptic one-liners," she muttered.

"Jenny, stop it." His voice was suddenly harsh. Jenny jumped a bit in surprise. "Just give me an answer," he went on. "I'll understand either way, but don't hide behind a wall of sarcasm, because I don't have the patience or the courage to cajole you."

Not yet, anyway, she answered him silently. But you will, if I have anything to say about it. "Where are the boys?" she asked suddenly, aiming for another chink in his armor.

Gage's voice sounded momentarily nonplussed. "In the family room watching a baseball game on the tube. Why?"

"Don't you suppose you ought to send them to a neighbor's or something just in case I accept? God knows, I don't want to be a bad influence on them." She knew it sounded silly, but it was no sillier than having him send the boys to the barbecue with his housekeeper on the Fourth of July.

"Jenny," he answered abruptly, roughly, "don't make this harder than it has to be."

"It doesn't have to be hard, Gage," she answered. "You're making it that way."

She half expected another crack about playing psychiatrist. Instead, he announced suddenly, "Danny's been asking about you."

More silence filled the telephone line. She thought it might suffocate her, but she refused to interrupt it. She sensed that he had something more to say.

"I've missed you, too," he finally continued, his voice subtly resigned again. Then he sighed, and his tone became harder. "We both know that I don't want it that way. We'd be fools if we tried to pretend that I'm overjoyed with the fact that I can't forget about you. I'm not. But I can't live with not seeing you, either." He paused. "Come over for dinner, Jenny Oliver. Let's talk about this."

Maybe, she thought, just maybe, she didn't have such an uphill climb ahead of her, after all. Jenny couldn't suppress a small smile of elation. It was a start, nothing more than that. But everything had to start somewhere. At least he wasn't immune to her.

"You can even wear Emilio Vasquente's clothes if you want. Hell, you can wear your French underwear, too."

She chuckled. "If you can hold those hot dogs for half an hour, you're on," she answered eventually, glancing down at her watch. Perfect timing, she thought. "Just give me a few minutes to get things straightened up around here."

"What about Kevin Washman?"

She'd nearly forgotten the lie. She floundered for a moment but recovered quickly, actually managing to use Gage's question to her best advantage. "Oh, him. Well, I've given him free reign with the wing. Whatever he wants to do with it is fine by me. I respect his judgment. I don't really have to be here to oversee things. He's just drawing up plans this afternoon, anyway."

His silence seemed disbelieving now—or was it just the sound of her own paranoia that she was hearing? He knew that she was too shrewd, too penurious with the business, to give a high-priced decorator free rein. If he thought about it enough, he'd know that she'd never hire a high-priced decorator for Timber House at this point, anyway. Not yet, she prayed. Don't let him catch on to me yet. I need more time to break through that resolve.

She interrupted his thoughts quickly before he had more time to think. "Don't tell me," she said drily. "Changing your mind already? Do me a favor this time and clam up on me now, not afterward. I think you were the one who pointed out that it's not fair to use me as a pawn."

It worked. His voice came back clipped. He was ready to spar with her again; he'd forgotten, if only momentarily, that she appeared to have lost her mind where the inn was concerned.

"I never change my mind, Jenny Oliver," he answered. "More often than not, I just come to my senses. See you in half an hour."

She hung up and wandered distractedly back into the lobby, her heart pounding. She'd planted the seeds. Now all she had to do was harvest the crop . . . carefully. She couldn't overdo it. He was too smart, knew her too well. One or two more well-aimed jabs, and then she'd leave him to stew. With any luck, he'd wake up and see what he was doing to himself, to them.

And without luck? She couldn't bear to think about it. If she failed this time, it would be the only failure that would ever matter, the only loss that would ever count. Ironically, she was betting everything—especially the heart she'd protected for so long—on the one thing about Gage Pierce that she wasn't sure of. She was gambling that he loved her. She was gambling that she could get through to him.

Her heart thundering, she went upstairs to her office to wait.

At exactly a quarter past five, one hour and ten minutes after Gage had called, Jenny pushed back her desk chair and got to her feet. Slowly, methodically, she went to the bathroom, brushed out her hair, and repaired what was left of her makeup. She stepped out of the skirt she wore and pulled on the new pair of jeans she'd bought the day before.

She was forty-five minutes late when she left Timber House, and she knew it would take her fifteen minutes or so to get to Gage's. An hour was what she had been aiming for, but it worked out better than she had dared to hope. Fate was on her side, she thought, watching as thunderous storm clouds floated in from the horizon. She glanced at them, then looked down at her watch, her stomach tightening nervously. It didn't take an idiot to know that Gage wouldn't be overjoyed with her excuse for being late. Better still, it was difficult to barbecue in the rain. He'd have every reason to be annoyed with her. With just a little help from the weather, she'd effectively disrupted the Pierces' dinner plans. And Danny would not only live, he would enjoy it.

As she pulled into Gage's driveway, the skies opened up with a torrential downpour. It took Gage so long to answer the doorbell that she began to wonder if he was even going to let her in to read her the riot act.

He answered just as she was about to ring again. One look at his face told that her plan had worked . . . so far.

His expression looked as though it had been carved in stone. His lips twisted into a taut frown, and his raven eyes were sharp and hard. He didn't even bother to say hello. "Do you want to tell them why we're having boiled hot dogs again," he asked, "or shall I?"

"I—" she began carefully, but he cut her off.

"Don't worry about it. They're used to it."

He didn't have to say it—the words were perfectly readable in his eyes. He considered it one of the bigger mistakes in his life that he had given her a second chance to get close to his children. Her throat closed and her head spun with stormy mixed emotions.

Guilt fairly swallowed her, but, by the same token, something defiant kept squirming deep inside her, too. She wasn't the only woman in the world who worked, and if they were all lynched for getting tied up at the office, the male race would be a damned lonely one. He, however, was undoubtedly the only man who would sacrifice his life for his son, without even trying to compromise. She couldn't hate him for it because she loved him for it. But she wasn't going to lose him for it. She met his accusing eyes with a slight tilt of her chin.

"Not from me, they're not," she answered sharply. "Do you want to give me a chance to make amends with them, or should I just go home?"

His mouth curved into a thin-lipped smile. "This I've got to see. By all means, come in and make amends." He stepped back to usher her inside with a theatrical flourish.

Jenny brushed past him, fixing him with a scowl before she made her way down the hallway.

"Tell them all about how very important the inn is and how you couldn't tear yourself away on time. They should be so captivated that they'll forget all about the hot dogs." His voice was a baiting undertone that dogged her footsteps as he followed her. Jenny whirled on her heel impulsively.

"Knock it off. I'm not going to go through a whole night of this. Just let me try to salvage dinner, and if you can't think of anything civil to say, then keep your mouth shut. The boys and I are going to have a good time. If you want to wallow in self-pity, then go ahead—but don't ruin *our* night!"

They froze and stared at each other. For a moment, Jenny's courage faltered as she held his eyes. Then she swallowed hard, straightened her spine, and turned back to the family room, leaving him standing in the foyer.

The sound of the television had led her to believe that the boys would be glued to the tube and virtually unaware of their aborted dinner plans, but she was wrong. Danny sat on the window seat, his desolate face pressed to the glass, while Ben stood stoically behind him, watching the downpour from a more dignified position. They both looked up at the sound of her footsteps. For a moment, guilt pressed in on her again. She was using them. But then, in a manner of speaking, so was Gage.

"Hi," she ventured.

They exchanged worried glances. "Did Dad call you so that we wouldn't have to have hot dogs again?" Ben asked after a moment.

"Are we gonna have to eat more of that beef str-stro-stuff?" Danny chimed in worriedly.

"It was all right, that beef stuff," Ben continued quickly. "He didn't mean that he didn't like it. I think he just likes hot dogs better." After a thoughtful pause, he admitted, "So do I."

Jenny lowered herself onto the sofa. "Well, don't worry. I'm not here to make that beef stuff." Danny's face brightened and he left the window seat to perch beside her. "And, actually, you two are saints. If you can say that you liked the stroganoff, then you're a lot more tactful than I am."

"What's tactful mean?" Danny asked.

"It means you're a good liar. The beef stroganoff was considerably overdone. The neighbor's dog might have liked it, but that's about it."

Ben started to giggle, then sobered. "If you're not here to make that, what are you going to do?" he asked suspiciously.

"Make hot dogs."

"But—"

"Yes, I know it's raining. But we can still barbecue them—sort of—if you'll help me." She was dimly aware of Gage's assessing expression as he finally arrived in the doorway, but she ignored him.

"How?" Ben took the bait without hesitation—for which she was immensely grateful.

"Well, I know you're Little Beach's most prized pitcher," she began. "But is either of you a Cub Scout?"

They looked at each other and shook their heads slowly. She wasn't sure if they had come to a mutual decision that she was out of her mind, or if they simply weren't scouts.

She frowned. "Oh. Well, I need a penknife of some kind."

Ben brightened suddenly. "I've got that! Dad takes us camping sometimes!"

Relief filtered through her. This was going to work, after all. "Okay," she answered. "You can be in charge of getting that, and Danny, I need you to go get your raincoat and an umbrella."

They were off in a flash, obviously believing that she could somehow stop the rain and save the day with penknives and raincoats. Gage, however, was a different matter entirely.

"What do you have up your sleeve?" he asked. There was a grudging respect in his voice but it didn't reach his eyes. They were vaguely suspicious. She knew he couldn't be catching on to her plan yet, but her pulse quickened in panic, anyway.

"Do you have a raincoat?" she asked abruptly without answering.

"Yes . . ." He drew the word out slowly, cautiously. "But I have to tell you that I'm not thrilled with the idea of going out in this rain. You'll have to give me a good reason if you want me to do it."

"No, I won't, because you don't have to go outside. All you have to do is lend me your raincoat."

They stared at each other in defiant silence for a moment, but he finally turned on his heel to do as she asked. Five minutes later, she and Danny were outside scouting the trees for likely looking branches.

When they brought them back inside, Ben handed her the penknife expectantly, but Gage only continued to watch her through dark, watchful eyes. She tried her best to ignore him as she shrugged out of his raincoat and left it in the mud room to dry.

"Okay," she announced, finally meeting his eyes in a silent challenge. "Now I need some newspaper."

"On the counter behind you." His voice was abrupt and factual. His eyes never left her.

If the boys noticed any of the tension between them, they didn't show it. Danny reached to hand her the newspaper and asked, "Now what?" His wide eyes were alive with intrigue. It occurred to Jenny briefly that perhaps she *should* have been a psychiatrist. He was reacting just as she had thought—and prayed—he would.

They spread the newspaper on the floor, and Ben helped her whittle the ends of the branches until they were sharp. Minutes later, they'd spread a blanket out on the floor in front of the fireplace and sat there holding their hot dogs out over the flames of a warming fire.

"This was a great idea," Danny enthused. So far, he'd put away two hot dogs and showed no signs of stopping, although Jenny expected that he was more enthralled with the art of cooking them than he was hungry.

"It was," Gage murmured from her side.

Jenny's eyes flew to his. He was smiling again, but this time the reflex was completely warm. Jenny felt her pulse lurch, then take off in a wild hum of happiness that was totally at odds with what she should have been feeling, considering the risk she was taking.

"The best part is that we won't have many dishes to wash," she answered when she trusted her voice.

But it wasn't true. The best part was his smile of approval.

Contrary to her forecast, however, cleaning up proved to be an all-night chore. The boys, knowing that the end of the job would mark their bedtime hour, stalled and procrastinated with their end of the chores. It was nearly ten o'clock when Gage finally came trotting down the stairs into the foyer with the news that they were in bed. Jenny looked out at him from her position on the parlor sofa with a relieved smile.

"I had no intention of lighting a fire under them. I just wanted to make sure that they had their hot dogs," she said, smiling.

He poured them fresh brandy and sat down beside her. "They were wound up tighter than drums," he answered in his familiar reserved, rusty voice. Then he turned his dark eyes on her, and more warmth crept into his tone. It made Jenny shiver with an almost uncomfortable feeling of hope and delight.

"They enjoyed the adventure of the whole thing," he went on. "So did I." Then he paused before adding, "That was pretty ingenious."

She took a careful sip of her brandy, feeling herself becoming unraveled by his praise and knowing that she couldn't afford to lose her composure now. "I think I got the idea from a book when I was a kid," she answered softly. "I told you that Ed used to work a lot and our plans together were often aborted. I remember thinking when I read about the old indoor-barbecue trick that it would have been nice if he could have done something that involved a little spontaneity once in a while, but unless I got underfoot at Timber House, he generally forgot I was around. That was the problem with Ed and me," she finished carefully. "It wasn't so much that he never spent much time with me. It was the fact that he didn't make the most of the time we did spend together. I didn't even understand until a few weeks ago that he loved me. I probably would have gone through my whole life not knowing if Mrs. Arnold hadn't been such a busybody and meddled in my affairs."

Gage was silent for a moment while he digested her words. She couldn't help hoping that he would finally understand that he wouldn't be robbing Danny if he went back to work, but only if he forgot how to be a father again. Instead, he replied, "I read that scheme somewhere, too. I just didn't think of doing it when the rain started." His look was suddenly speculative again. "What happened at the inn to make you so late?"

She swallowed hard and forced the lie. "The usual. Washman was late, and I at least wanted to be there to greet him. Derrick Caide called in sick, and I had to man the front desk until Sally could come in to cover for him. It was no big deal. I still had some phone calls to make to set up that charity thing, so I was able to use the time."

His gaze returned to her sharply. She could see him trying to fight his sense of satisfaction. "You're going to do that after all, hmm?"

Jenny shrugged. He wasn't going to live vicariously through her—not if she had anything to say about it. "It was a brilliant idea. You are a genius, Gage, even if you did start out as an unwanted partner."

She expected his frown. Actually, she was banking on it. "I've made a few little changes in the original idea, of course," she went on. "But then, I'm aiming for more dramatic results."

He shot her a wary look as he refilled her brandy, then got up to poke at the embers in the fireplace. "In what way?"

"Well, the idea for the historical society was good, but who makes up the historical society? A bunch of old women from Longport City, Brookings, and a handful of other towns on the mainland. Their days for throwing wedding receptions and whatnot are waning, not to mention the fact that they wouldn't be likely to use Timber House at any rate. It's doubtful that they'd go through the hassle of using the ferry when they've got a bumper crop of banquet facilities on the mainland."

He glanced back at her over his shoulder. "Something tells me you're thinking too much, Jenny Oliver."

She shrugged carelessly. "Well, it makes sense to me. Why aim this charity idea at a group that's not going to yield results? And why go for charity at all? Why not just throw a huge open house for the people on the island? *They're* the ones who are going to use our banquet facilities if they're impressed."

He straightened slowly and returned to her. His midnight gaze was unreadable. Her heart lurched. "Sure," he agreed evenly. "Except for one thing. An open house will cost a hell of a lot more than a small charitable function. You're talking about a difference of maybe fifty people versus a thousand. Where are you going to get the money without putting the inn even further in the red?"

"I—" she began, then broke off at the look in his eyes.

He knew. He knew what she was trying to do. She was suddenly and dreadfully sure of it.

He shook his head slowly. "No, Jenny Oliver, I won't buy it. You're not stupid. You're too damned good at what you do. You know you're not running the Warwick any longer, that you're not working with a virtually unlimited budget. You're up to something." Suddenly, roughly, he reached down and pulled her to her feet.

"What?" he demanded. "What is it?"

His voice was harsh, his anger barely controlled. Sheer, black fright swept through her, darker and more desperate than anything she had ever known. He shook her once, quickly and hard, as though to jar the answer out of her. She'd never seen him like this before. For one breathless, terrifying moment, she wondered if he was going to get violent, but that didn't frighten her half as much as the fact that she had gambled and lost . . . and that she would surely lose him.

But instead of shaking her again, he reached out to trail a finger down her jaw with sweet intent. Jenny stiffened briefly in surprise, her wide gray eyes jumping to his. Understanding came to her slowly, pushing through the befuddled panic in her brain. His black eyes burned with wanting again, asking her for something that she had never been able to deny him.

"I warned you once, Jenny Oliver," he went on huskily. "You're no match for me. I don't know what you're up to, but I know what you've done."

"You . . . you do?" Her voice was disappearing again, just the way it always did when he was too near. And now she was grappling with more than just his proximity. She was trying to figure out what he was thinking. For once, she didn't know.

"You've been watching me all night with those burning quicksilver eyes." His hand found her chin and turned her head to face him just when she had finally forced herself to look away. "Watching . . . and waiting, maybe?" His fingers traced her lips now, softly and seductively. "For what? For this? To see if you could get to me again? Is that part of the scheme?"

"Get to you?" she repeated, her voice a strangled whisper.

"It worked."

Oh, no, it didn't, she thought wildly. This wasn't what she had bargained for, wasn't the result that she had been praying for. But she didn't protest when he lowered his mouth to hers and kissed her. Instead, she felt herself melting as his fingers found their way into her hair. Her panic and fear were drowned beneath an assault of yearning.

"It always works when you look at me like that," he went on, his voice husky. She shuddered convulsively as the sound of it made a delicious, dangerous warmth cascade through her. She knew that she should stop him; he was only offering her the things that were easiest for him to give. He wasn't offering himself, and that was the one thing she so desperately needed— that was her goal. Yet she couldn't refuse his touch and the soft, sweet, honest side of him that had always rocked her soul.

He was so many different men, and that had been what had captured her intrigue when he'd first stormed into her life. But now, months later, she knew that it was this softer side of him that she loved the most . . . the side of him that bound his entire world to Danny, the side that had urged him to help Ed . . . the part that kept him from giving all of himself to her.

The thought should have helped her to resist his tender assault, but it didn't. She didn't *want* to resist it. Suddenly, she needed him to want her as painfully and as completely as she wanted him. All her other weapons had failed. She hadn't been able to shake him up enough to make him realize that he needed to work as badly as Danny needed him . . . that he *wanted* to work, and work with her. But she still had one last tool in her arsenal.

She had her love for him.

She held his mouth with her own and slid trembling fingers through his dark hair. She kissed him slowly, savoring the feel of his mouth against hers, trying to tell him what she couldn't tell him with words . . . that he was her world.

Her hands slid down to his shoulders, and without consciously realizing what she was doing, she drew him back toward the sofa. As they tumbled down upon it, she parted her lips against his, silently pleading with him to do the same and deepen their kiss. He did, pushing her back against the cushions, his weight coming down atop her in hot, sweet hunger.

He made a sound deep in his throat as his arms came around her, so strong and so possessive. An odd mixture of security and desire danced through her at his embrace. She burrowed more deeply into his arms as they tightened around her, then softened, melting into him.

He was being a gentle lover again, a man who sought to please her more than he wanted to please himself. The realization that he could be like that never failed to stun her, and she gasped softly as he kissed the corners of her mouth and the pulse beating at her throat. His mouth was like a butterfly, lighting in a new place whenever she least expected it. He found her eyelids, the edge of her ear, her lips again. Jenny sighed softly, clinging to him.

His response to her sigh was a vague shuddering, and she understood suddenly how much it was costing him to go slowly. The realization reassured her and gave her the courage to love him more completely . . . if only silently. She gloried in the intimate caress of his tongue against hers even as she tried to push him to give up his restraint. She met his mouth more demandingly until she sensed something snapping inside him and his kiss began to consume her.

Familiar fire began to lick through her. She arched into him, making it almost impossible for him to free the buttons of the sweater she wore, but somehow he accomplished the task. When she was free of the confining knit, his hands danced over her skin, moving delicately from her breasts to her waist. They elicited from her a response even more thunderous than any she had ever felt before. She gasped again, her eyes flying open to be met by his ebony ones. Mere moments ago, he had seemed so dangerously angry, she thought, so hard and violent and unforgiving. Now, he was so incredibly gentle that she had never felt more cherished.

His mouth found the tip of her breast and she shuddered deliciously, feeling an answering tremor in his body that meant more than his touch. It told her that he was vulnerable to her, too, and that was something that she needed desperately to know. She groaned again at the fiery sensation of his tongue teasing her nipple, and her hands clutched his shoulders in a silent demand for more. The heat that suffused her became almost unbearable as his hand found her other breast and his fingers brushed that nipple slowly until it was coaxed into hardness as well.

She couldn't stand it much longer. She needed the fulfillment of him, needed it before she was scorched by the sizzling yearning inside her. But this time his lovemaking was different still from the times before, and he seemed hesitant to give her the release she so needed. As she writhed beneath him, his mouth roamed slowly between her breasts and he tortured her with a patience that she knew he couldn't possibly be feeling.

His mouth came back to hers, capturing it in another kiss that was as deep as the sea that banked the island. Then, finally, he pulled away from her and slid her jeans down her body. She was torn between a desire for him to come back to her and another that wanted him to get out of his own clothes. It seemed like forever before he returned to enfold her in his arms, but just when she thought he would fill her again in the way she'd been dreaming of, he shifted his weight against the back of the sofa instead. His eyes coasted down over her nakedness, showing silent approval of the way her skin gleamed with a transparent hint of the moonlight that drifted through the window.

"Yes, you are the brightest flame," he whispered throatily, finally, "and I just can't seem to resist you. I want to, but God, I just can't."

She started to answer, but then her voice caught almost painfully in her throat. His hand slid over her skin again, but this time it kept moving until he was exploring her more fully than he ever had before. His fingers found the warmth between her thighs and touched her slowly until she cried out again. Still, he wouldn't release her from the building, hungry torment that claimed her. He shifted his weight once more until his tongue followed the trail of his hands. Jenny twisted beneath him until the warmth inside her began to gather toward explosion, and she prayed that this time he would finally let it happen.

He did. She barely had time to gasp his name before he took her breath away one last time. She opened her eyes slowly, dazed by the sweet restraint of his loving. He loomed above her now, his body looking taut and strong in the milky moonlight. His eyes were the shining black stones that she had always likened them to, but now they weren't flat. They were as alive and as fiery as the passion that scorched through her.

When he finally pushed into her, pleasure exploded through her body instantaneously. It was followed by the first craved beginnings of release. Finally, she shuddered in his arms and felt him give in to his own needs and desires. He groaned her name softly and amazingly tenderly.

It was a long time before either one of them risked speaking. And then he spoke the only words in the English language that could destroy the hope she'd finally allowed herself to feel.

"I'm sorry," he whispered.

10

Jenny felt her heart roll over sickly as she looked up at him. With her lips still burning from the imprint of his kiss, her body still full and faintly throbbing from his loving, she found that her brain simply refused to accept what she had heard. But her body didn't. Nausea, sharp and sudden, twisted in her stomach and her palms turned sweaty.

Calm down, she instructed herself desperately. Think. He's said two words. Don't react until you have the full story. Even feeling as drugged and overwhelmed as she did, she knew that to deal with this man impulsively was too dangerous to be considered.

Gage braced his weight against the back of the sofa as he ran a hand through his hair and let out a ragged sigh. Then, suddenly, he pushed away from her and got to his feet. Too suddenly, she thought. A premonition of impending disaster trembled through her as she took in his expression.

"Sorry?" she managed to say, then paused to clear her throat. "For what?"

Gage pulled his jeans on and moved to the window without answering. Then, just as Jenny began to wonder if he was going to ignore her question, his voice floated back to her, rough and anguished. "I wasn't going to let that happen tonight."

Jenny bristled—and was grateful for the instinctive response. She clung to it as her only armor against what was happening. "I see," she answered shortly. "Well, you *never* intend to let it happen, and you've never apologized before. Turning over a new leaf, Gage? Do apologies help you assuage your guilt? If that's the case, then you ought to be all squared away with Danny. You've been apologizing to him for five years and destroying yourself in the process."

She didn't know what made her say it. Anger, perhaps, and hurt—and fear that she was going to lose him, after all. She more than half expected that he would respond in fury, and she braced herself for it, but he was a different man now, one whom she didn't know.

"I have to talk to you," he said instead.

"Gage, don't," she pleaded in a whisper, her anger suddenly gone. She moved to sit up. "Whatever it is, think about it first. Don't say anything until you've thought it out." I'm not sure I can handle it, she finished silently. Don't make me until I absolutely have to.

"Think about it?" he scoffed, his voice suddenly hard. "I *have* thought about it. Constantly. Since the day I first got off that elevator and found out that the woman I was following was Jenny Oliver. It's just taken me this long to do something about it."

Jenny stared at him dully, her heart pounding painfully at his words. She knew what he was going to say and wanted to fight it, but she couldn't seem to find the fledgling irritation that had claimed her so briefly a moment before. She wanted to feel angry that she had lost. All she could feel was despair.

Gage didn't seem to notice her uncharacteristic silence. He poured himself some brandy and leaned back against the wall near the fireplace with another frustrated sigh. "I asked you to come over tonight so that we could talk about this . . . this . . . whatever the hell it is that's happening between us. I thought we could shrug and chuckle like two modern-day adults and say, 'Oh, well, it didn't work for us. Let's shake hands and be friends.' Then you walked in here and made Danny's face light up like a Christmas tree, started playing crazy games with me about the hotel, started looking at me with that way you have—" He broke off. "Hell, Jenny!" he said gruffly. "I can't take this! You're more than I can stand!"

It would have been ironic had it not been so heart-rending. She had gambled that he would be vulnerable to her. He was. Too much so, if what he seemed to be saying was any indication. If she had been herself, she would have had to fight off the urge to laugh hysterically. But she wasn't herself. With a small moan of distress, she jumped to her feet again and started grabbing her clothes.

Gage's voice stopped her. It was sinking anguish more than curiosity that made her pause and turn back to him.

"No!" His voice cracked through the room like a whip. "You're not leaving. I've given too much effort to working myself up to this point for you to walk out now. Pour yourself a drink, sit down, and listen to me. At least give me the satisfaction of speaking the words, even if I didn't have the guts to do it when I should have." Suddenly, his tone was raw, unbearably ashamed and self-recriminating. It got to her like nothing else could have.

She took a few deep breaths to steady herself, then returned to the sofa. She kept her back to him while she dressed, then sat down carefully, perching on the edge with her hands clenched tightly in her lap. "I don't want anything to drink," she managed to say quietly. "Just . . . just tell me what you wanted to talk to me about." His expression left her no doubt that it wasn't going to be good. She wondered wildly how much more of this she could stand.

He turned his back on her to pour himself another drink. He'd polished the last one off with one long swallow. "I've waited two months for you to get around to buying out my share of the inn," he began tightly. "I can't wait anymore, Jenny."

Jenny's eyes flew to his as he turned around. Oddly, she was grateful for the topic of conversation, but then, her senses were dulled with panic and she wasn't thinking clearly. She didn't see that his words were just storm clouds building. She thought that the issue was relatively easy to settle. You couldn't get blood out of a rock, she thought, and she didn't have the money with which to buy him out. She got to her feet again.

"Oh, that," she answered. "Just give me a little more time. I don't have the money to buy you out right now. I'll have to fly back to California and take out a loan. Sorry," she finished emptily. "There's nothing else I can do for you at the moment."

"Sure there is."

She stopped dead in her tracks again as she reached the door, then looked back at him. "Pardon me?"

"There *is* something else you can do," he explained, his voice growing even more strained. "I've given this a great deal of thought in the last few weeks. You might not be able to buy me out, but I can buy you out. I *do* have the cash, and I think it would be wisest for both of us if I used it."

"Wisest for both of us?" she echoed softly.

"That's right." He started out evenly enough, but then something seemed to snap inside him. "Damn it, Jenny, I can't stay away from you! Don't you see that? I can't stand running into you in grocery stores, and I don't need to live with the knowledge that you're living a quarter of a mile away, because I can't stay away from you. I want you to leave. Go back to San Francisco. Leave Timber House to me. I promise you I won't sell out to International. Someone else. Someone small, who'll do what you're doing. But not you. Not someone I've got to watch, knowing all along that we'd be an unbeatable team, that we—" He broke off, controlling himself. "No. It can't happen, and I don't have the willpower to stop it if you stay. Please, Jenny, if you feel anything for me at all, then go away. Go back to Warwick Towers. Let me stay here and do what I have to do for Danny in peace."

His words sank in on her slowly. The swell of pain and defeat inside her as she understood was almost beyond tears.

Almost, but not quite. She blinked wildly against the urge to cry and stared at him. It never occurred to her that she had once believed that he was only willing to continue seeing her because he wasn't in love with her. She only knew that he wanted her out of his life. Ice seemed to settle into her every pore with the knowledge, and she hugged herself against an involuntary shiver.

She'd lost him. His guilt over Danny was too strong, stronger than she was, stronger than he was. She couldn't fight it.

Gage didn't notice her stricken expression. He turned away to refill his glass yet again, speaking to her over his shoulder. His voice was steadier now.

"Think about it, Jenny. That's all I ask. It's the perfect alternative. You haven't wanted to be here from the start. You wanted to be back in California, playing with all your marbles, to quote you directly. So go. I'm giving you the opportunity to do it. You could even use the money from the sale to open your own hotel there." He turned back to her suddenly, polishing off his drink and setting his glass down hard on a nearby table. "There's no reason for you to hang around Little Beach any longer," he announced, his voice suddenly hard. She didn't hear the desperation in it, only the finality. "Our relationship is never going to go anywhere, right? We can keep circling each other and hanging on to our respective shares of Timber House until we're blue in the face, but all it's going to do is hurt both of us. So let's do the kindest thing for ourselves and part ways. Little Beach is just too small to hold the two of us. I like it here, you don't, so the issue is really pretty clear-cut as to who should leave and who should stay."

She barely heard his words for the whirling thoughts in her own brain. He didn't want her. She'd failed. Lost. She cringed inwardly as she thought of what she had always considered to be her other failures. How little she had known about losing then, she thought desperately. How little she had known about this depth of defeat. She closed her eyes, her heart aching in pain as she backed toward the door.

"I . . . I'll have to think about it," she said in a strangled voice. "I . . . I can't make a decision now, I can't . . ." She trailed off, swallowing convulsively. Swallowing the sob that rose in her throat, she turned on her heel and ran.

She'd chosen to make the long trip to San Francisco by car that night when she'd run from Gage's house, from his words, from him. Now, approaching the dock on the ferry, she was immensely glad that she had.

Jenny had known herself well enough to know that the best thing she could have done for herself that night was to get out of Little Beach immediately—just as she had understood that she'd need every minute of the long drive back today to brace herself for seeing him again. She'd known that she'd never be able to cope with or make a decision regarding his proposal while living in Ed's house, while seeing Timber House every day. And she knew that she'd never be able to face Gage today without a lot of time to steel herself for the ordeal.

As she drove off the ferry, her movements were rigid with iron self-control. Her soft features were grim but steady. She drove quickly, but that was part of the plan. She knew that the only way she was going to get through this day was to devise a strict mental outline of what she had to do and adhere to it rigidly and rapidly. No matter what happened, she would be calm. No matter what happened, she would not cry.

When she arrived at the cottage, she didn't allow herself the luxury of looking it over one last time. She got out of the Mercedes, her head bowed, studiously watching the path of her feet as she made her way up onto the porch. Inside, she spent two hours methodically and carefully packing up the possessions she had accumulated there, then moved to Ed's bedroom.

Her stiff control fled for a fraction of a second as she pushed open the door. This would be the easy part of the job . . . if only because she had prepared for it. But she had separated Ed's most precious possessions from the mundane ones during those early weeks in Little Beach with the intention of clearing out quickly when the time came for her to return to San Francisco. Now the time had come, and she no longer wanted to go.

She wanted to stay in Little Beach. And she couldn't. As Gage had said, the island wasn't big enough to hold both of them.

She shook her head fiercely, refusing to think about it, then bent over the closet floor in Ed's bedroom. All the items that she had packed nearly three months ago were there. She slid the boxes out and nudged them out to the front door with her foot.

When it was all over, she went into the sitting room and poured herself a single brandy. It was the only fortification she would allow herself. She had to do this with a clear head; she couldn't risk getting emotional.

Then she was ready.

She made the telephone call, not speaking with Gage, but merely determining that he was at the inn. She had known that he would be; without her agreement, he couldn't have sold the place yet, and *somebody* had to run it until he could. Then she made a second call, gathering neighborhood teen-agers to help her with the boxes. She didn't look back at the cottage as they loaded the boxes into her car. She paid them and locked up emotionlessly, then started to scout the yard for the cat.

Mrs. Arnold's voice proved to be the first chink in her armor. She wasn't supposed to be part of the routine. She had no role in the plan. Jenny had even avoided the necessity of bringing Chesterfield to her, intending instead to leave the quarrelsome cat on Gage's doorstep. She didn't want to face Rosemary Arnold any more than she wanted to go away without leaving Gage with a last, childish piece of revenge.

She'd just collected the cat from a sunny spot on the back porch when the old woman called out to her from the other side of the fence.

"I feed him while you're gone. I don't exactly take care of him. I've come to the conclusion that that's impossible. He takes care of himself, roaming the neighborhood at will. When did you get back?"

The question was so idle that Jenny had no doubt that it was loaded.

"A few hours ago," she answered briefly, afraid to stop to talk to her, afraid to deviate from her plan. She didn't have the strength or the courage to go it alone without some sort of prearranged schedule.

"And now you're leaving," the woman announced too conversationally. "I saw you loading the boxes into your car. Where are you taking them? What are you doing with Chesterfield?" she finished, watching the ludicrous spectacle of Jenny trying to get him into a cat carrier.

"To Gage," she responded without looking up. She didn't dare. Then she snapped "Damn!" as a claw sank into the fleshy pad of her finger. She stuck it in her mouth and kept wrestling with him.

"This should prove interesting." She wasn't talking about Chesterfield's reaction to the cat carrier, and Jenny knew it. She looked up at the old woman suddenly, her expression desperate.

"Please, don't," she blurted out. "I have to do this."

Amazingly, the old woman shrugged. "I know. It'll come full circle, but you have to go through the motions." She looked at Jenny shrewdly. "You're planning to sell the cottage and Timber House, as well?"

Jenny stared at her helplessly. The old woman wasn't going to make this any easier for her. "I'm going to sell my half of Timber House to Gage. And I've listed the cottage with a realtor in Longport City." She knew it would be simplest to just supply the woman with the information she was looking for and get it over with.

She remained silently watchful as Jenny shoved Chesterfield gingerly into the carrier, snapped the door closed before he could escape, and carried him out to the car. A long, steady howl reverberated throughout the neighborhood as Mrs. Arnold followed her progress along the fence.

Then the woman's wrinkled face creased into a smile. Jenny felt a stab of pain pierce through her heart. How was she ever going to be able to say good-bye to her? If only she had stayed away, if only she hadn't come outside to talk just this once. She opened her mouth, determined to force the farewells, no matter how painful it might prove to be, but Mrs. Arnold cut her off.

"There's no need to say good-bye," she announced. "You'll be back." With that, she turned and toddled off in the direction of her house again.

Oh, no, I won't, Jenny thought silently, desperately. Not this time. She considered following her to tell her so, to tell her good-bye, then took the coward's way out. Brushing away her sudden tears so that she could see, she turned back to the car. She dropped Chesterfield's carrier in the passenger's seat, then climbed in herself. Her fingers trembled as she tried to fit the key into the ignition.

When the engine finally caught, a sob caught in her throat as well, but she battled it back. She turned in the direction of Timber House, girding herself for the last half—the hardest half by far—of the plan.

She carried only the cat carrier up to the fifth floor. She had two of the bellboys leave the rest of the boxes in Horace's office. Another pain lashed into her heart as she considered the fact that Horace wouldn't protest, even if Gage left them there for a year. He'd step quietly around them every day without uttering a word of complaint.

She didn't want to run into anyone else on her way up to the office, and she didn't. She reached the door to Ed's old office and pushed it open unceremoniously.

Gage glanced up from the desk at the intrusion, a dark frown of disapproval on his face until he recognized her. Then his expression smoothed out into the perfect noncommittal gaze that she knew so well.

Jenny felt her throat closing up and her body beginning to tremble. It took everything she had to steel herself to meet those raven eyes. She moved to the center of the room and dropped the cat carrier on the floor.

"That's not . . ." Gage began, then trailed off.

"It is."

"Are you trying to be spiteful?"

"You've got it." Her voice was strong and steady, but she had to wonder how much longer it would hold out. Best to get this over with quickly, she thought as panic began to grip her. Pain, fresh and aching, was welling up inside her insidiously at the torture of seeing him again.

Gage was on his feet in an instant, his features darkening into another formidable scowl. "Jenny, for God's sake, what are you

178

up to? I don't want the damned cat. What am I supposed to do—take him home and feed him Danny and Ben for dinner?"

"Only if you don't have any fresh salmon on hand."

He gave her a withering glance, then picked the carrier up gingerly and put it on the desk. Chesterfield hissed from inside.

"The other stuff's down in Horace's office. The boxes are heavy and I couldn't carry them upstairs. The bellboys were busy, so I just told them to leave them there until you decided what to do with them. My last official order," she rushed on quickly, desperate to get the words out and leave before she fell apart. "It's all that nautical stuff that you noticed missing the first day you came here." The reference to that day almost undid her, but she swallowed hard and pushed on. "It all meant a lot to Ed, as I'm sure you know, so I thought it belonged here. I'm planning to sell the rest of the stuff with the house."

He looked at her blankly. "You're selling the house?"

"And the inn. It's yours. I've decided to accept your offer. I've notified my lawyers. If you'll just contact them, they'll handle everything for me."

She felt him stiffen rather than saw him do it. Suddenly, an electric tension was in the air. Jenny started moving toward the door instinctively, a wild fear claiming her at the thought of what that tension could do to her resolve.

His voice rang out like a gunshot, stopping her. "You're going back to San Francisco?" he demanded.

"Of course." Gone was her steadiness. Her voice sounded uneven. "It's what you wanted, if I remember correctly."

"What I wanted," he repeated hollowly. He looked tired, she thought. She supposed that the inn had been pretty busy. But then, with her talent to start it and his to finish it, why not? She flinched away from the thought, afraid to consider what might have been if things had worked out differently.

"I think that covers everything," she rushed on. "I—I've got to run. It's a long drive back to San Francisco, and I want to do it tonight." She didn't tell him that she couldn't bear staying in Little Beach one second more than she had to, knowing that he was so close.

"Back? Is that where you've been?"

She nodded quickly, taking another step backward toward the door.

"I tried to find you. I called the Warwick, but they told me that they hadn't heard from you." He was watching her with that same expression he had worn so often back in the early days when he had always been trying to assess her.

"I stayed with friends."

He nodded slowly. "Well, it doesn't matter. I knew you had to come back eventually, and you're here now. Can we talk?"

"No!" The single word was hysterical and quick. It was the last thing she wanted, the one thing she knew she wouldn't be able to get through. "No," she murmured again. "Please, you've said enough. I've got to go. Call my lawyers with anything else you need to discuss."

She didn't wait for him to answer. With a desperate look, she bolted out the door. She had no choice. She couldn't stay. She was falling apart. It was in the trembling of her knees, in the tears burning hotly behind her eyes, and the nauseous clenching of her stomach.

She couldn't bear the sight of him any longer.

Her path was instinctive, although it hadn't been part of her original plan. She hadn't wanted to go through any maudlin good-byes to Little Beach or the inn. She had wanted to hit town and run. No messing with memories, no unleashed emotions. Yet she veered sharply to the right after she left the office, anyway, and plunged through the door to the widow's walk, taking the old steps recklessly two at a time. She didn't see the cobwebs laced against the corners of the stairs or smell the damp mustiness of virtually unused air. She hurried to the top and collapsed against the seaside wall, dropping down onto the floor and cradling her head on her knees.

And then she cried.

She wept aloud, finally and fully, her sobs racking her insides. She cried for Gage and for herself, for the island home she was losing just when she realized that it *was* home, and for the loss of love. She never heard his footsteps on the stairs. She sat in the place she had spent hours in as a child, yielding to the sobs that shook her.

"You were right. I was torturing myself with guilt. What was more, I was driving Danny and Ben crazy."

She lifted her head at the sound of his voice and glanced up at him dully, sniffing slightly but saying nothing. He stood against the railing, a Poseidon against the backdrop of the sea. The wind ruffled his dark hair, and the brightness of the sky made his eyes look like gleaming onyx.

She wondered how she was ever going to bear losing him.

"Is that what you were trying to do that night?" he went on. She only blinked in response. "When you were telling me all that crazy crap about decorators and open houses?"

She stiffened at the tension in his voice. "I know," she answered abruptly, finally speaking. "I lied. It was the only way I could think of to—" She broke off quickly as tears began to clog her throat again. "Nothing ventured, nothing gained," she finished, struggling to her feet.

His voice stopped her just as she got leverage. "Jenny, I'm not angry." Gage sighed. She sank back against the wall again, finding she had no more energy to run with. "I'm just sorry it didn't work."

"So am I," she whispered raggedly. "Sorry, but not surprised."

"Then."

"What?" She glanced up at him in exhausted confusion.

"I said I'm sorry it didn't work then. It might have spared us the hell of the last two weeks."

She didn't understand. "Nothing could have spared us, Gage," she answered wearily. "We've been hurtling toward hell like a runaway train ever since you first walked into Ed's office with that partnership agreement."

"And maybe we could come back again if you'd just shut up and listen to me!" His voice was suddenly sharp. Jenny jumped slightly, her eyes flying to his and fixing on him widely.

"What?" she demanded again.

"I'm trying to tell you that you were right! And that maybe your little plot didn't work, but you succeeded anyway!"

"Yeah, and I can tell you're real pleased about it!"

"For God's sake, Jenny, what are you talking about?"

"That's just it! I'm talking. You're shouting. Don't yell at me, Gage!"

Silence fell between them suddenly. As the roar of the surf crashed around them, Jenny realized almost distantly that she wasn't shaking anymore. And she wasn't fighting tears anymore. She squinted up at him. "What did you say?" she whispered.

His slow grin spread over his mouth. "You must be hard of hearing if you didn't hear me the first time."

"Must be."

"I'm sorry I yelled at you. You're so damned hotheaded sometimes."

"Most of the time. With you, anyway. Don't be sorry. Just tell me again."

His grin faded. He shrugged. "As soon as you gave up trying to hatch insidious little plots against me, you succeeded. Abandoning me with Timber House for two weeks and making me go back to work did the job nicely and easily. I woke up and saw what you were trying to make me see . . . that I'd retired out of guilt . . . that Danny and Ben didn't need me around twenty-four hours a day . . . that *I* just needed to be with them to repent for what I'd done to them all those years ago." He chuckled shortly. "Kids. When I finally got around to talking to them about it, they told me I was driving them crazy. Anyway, you were right. I was overcompensating. There was no need to retire. I just can't work like a maniac. But then, I don't have to anymore. I've got a partner now."

She stared at him blankly, a small frown furrowing between her eyebrows. Deep in her chest, her heart skipped a beat, then broke into a thunderous rhythm, but the only outward sign of it was the small gasp she gave.

His voice grew tight again at her lack of response. "Well, don't I?"

"What?"

"Have a partner, damn it!"

"I don't know. That depends."

He gave her a wary look. "On what?"

She sighed shakily. "Gage, I . . . I'm very glad that you don't have to torture yourself into retirement anymore. But that only solves things between you and the hotel. It doesn't do a damned thing for you and me."

His eyebrows rose incredulously. "Jenny, for God's sake, I'm baring my soul to you! Can't you read a little between the lines?" Suddenly, he scowled. "No. No, you won't do that. You want it all spelled out. Okay. I'm sorry I blamed you for making me think about working again." His voice softened. "Jenny, I'm sorry. We both know it was me and not you. *I* wanted to go back to work. I just couldn't admit it to myself until you came along and forced me to. And I was scared to death because I wanted you . . . and I haven't wanted a woman since this whole thing started. I was fighting myself and blaming you for making me do it."

His voice was suddenly tired. Jenny scrambled to her feet and took a single step closer to him, both wanting to comfort him and pour out her love for him, and wanting to run.

"Don't go, Jenny. Stay here. I don't want to buy you out. I want to be partners. I want to go for the marbles again. With you."

She swallowed hard before trusting herself to speak. "Are you rescinding your offer?"

"Just making a new one."

He spoke the words softly, but they screamed their way into her heart. The last weak threads of her control snapped.

Before she knew what she was doing, she was in his arms. He held her tightly, almost desperately, as fresh tears slid down her cheeks. She clung to him senselessly long after his first chuckles began to ripple through the hardness of his body.

"You've got to stay," he went on. "You can't leave me with that damned cat."

Jenny pulled away from him enough to glance up at him with a tremulous smile, her face still glistening with her tears.

"Look at it this way," Gage continued. "If you leave him here, he'll have the hotel in the red again in no time. Guests don't like to be terrorized."

She laughed shakily, then sobered abruptly. "Oh, God," she moaned softly. "Gage, we can't do this. I can't stay on the basis of a disreputable cat, and you know it."

The look he gave her was burning and intent. It flushed her with heat, even as she forced herself to look away from him.

"And," she forced herself to continue, "the only thing worse than staying together because of the cat would be staying together to save Timber House."

There was a long, heavy pause. Her breath seemed to lodge painfully in her throat as she waited for his answer. She knew what she wanted it to be, what she ached for it to be, and was afraid to hope.

And then, eventually, he said the words she longed to hear. "How about if we stay together because we love each other? Does that pass muster?"

A brilliant smile of relief touched her lips. Joy bubbled in her laugh and gleamed in her eyes. "It might," she answered.

"Ah, but then I'm doing it to you again."

She scowled. "Doing what?"

"Expecting things of you."

"Like what?"

"I'm just assuming that we love each other. You've never told me that you love me, Jenny Oliver."

A small sigh of relief escaped her. Her answering grin made her face shine as she found her way back into his arms again. "Oh, that."

"Oh, that," he repeated slowly. "That's it?"

"I love you, Gage Pierce," she whispered, suddenly serious again as she looked up at him. "I have from the first moment I realized that you weren't so proper and controlled that you couldn't do something outrageous—like save me from a very boring dinner date with Colby Barrett." Suddenly, she laughed again, a bright, delighted sound. "You were so suave and unperturbed about what you'd done! And it shook me to the bottom of my toes."

"Well, I'm not suave and unperturbed right now."

She searched his eyes, confused by the almost tight edge that had crept into his voice again. "Why not?"

"Because I'm still waiting for your answer."

"My answer? Oh, you mean: Will I stay? Do you mean to tel

me that you haven't guessed that I up until two weeks ago, I never intended to go?"

His eyes were dark and stormy. "I'd hoped. But I don't want to have to hope now. I want to know. There's more involved than just staying in Little Beach, Jenny Oliver. I want to know that you'll stay for good."

She wasn't sure what he wanted from her. She bit her lip. "Well, you might consider tying me to the bedpost," she joked, deciding humor was the best option.

But Gage didn't smile. His look was intense and serious. "What I had in mind was tying you to me," he answered. "Marry me, Jenny."

Her smile broadened again. "In a minute," she answered. "Like I told you, I want all the marbles."

"All of them?" he repeated, echoing her emphasis on the first word.

"Not just the inn. Not just a business partner. You," she clarified softly. "All of you. All of it."

His answering smile was wide, and it was designed to rattle her again. "That should be easy enough to take care of. Should we take them in order? Let's start with the inn. There's a wedding reception scheduled in the banquet room for Saturday. I'm sure the staff can use all the help they can get." He made a move toward the stairs. "Shall we?"

She gave him a mischievous look as she led the way. "No, thanks," she murmured.

He feigned a look of surprise. "What's this I hear? Jenny Oliver turning down a chance to go for all the marbles? She must have other things on her mind."

She didn't answer until they reached the fourth floor. "You've just got the order of my marbles all mixed up," she responded. "Allow me to help you get them straightened out." She glanced around the corridor with a wide grin. "Which room's empty?"

"Four-ten. What—?" Before he could continue she pushed open the door and pulled him inside. As she knocked the door closed with her foot, she sought his mouth with hers.

"Oh, *those* marbles," he teased. It took only another moment of her tender assault before he sobered again, then eased her down on the bed. His eyes warmed the deepest part of her soul.

"I love you, Jenny Pierce," he whispered, then leaned up on his elbow to give her one last smile. "Hmm. It has a nice ring."

WIN
a fabulous $50,000 diamond jewelry collection

by filling out the coupon below and mailing it by September 30, 1985

Send entries to:

U.S.
Silhouette Diamond Sweepstakes
P.O. Box 779
Madison Square Station
New York, NY 10159

Canada
Silhouette Diamond Sweepstakes
Suite 191
238 Davenport Road
Toronto, Ontario M5R 1J6

SILHOUETTE DIAMOND SWEEPSTAKES
ENTRY FORM

☐ Mrs. ☐ Miss ☐ Ms ☐ Mr.

NAME   (please print)

ADDRESS   APT. #

CITY

STATE/(PROV.)

ZIP/(POSTAL CODE)

RTD-A-1

RULES FOR SILHOUETTE DIAMOND SWEEPSTAKES

OFFICIAL RULES—NO PURCHASE NECESSARY

1. Silhouette Diamond Sweepstakes is open to Canadian (except Quebec) and United States residents 18 years or older at the time of entry. Employees and immediate families of the publishers of Silhouette, their affiliates, retailers, distributors, printers, agencies and RONALD SMILEY INC. are excluded.

2. To enter, print your name and address on the official entry form or on a 3" x 5" slip of paper. You may enter as often as you choose, but each envelope must contain only one entry. Mail entries first class in Canada to Silhouette Diamond Sweepstakes, Suite 191, 238 Davenport Road, Toronto, Ontario M5R 1J6. In the United States, mail to Silhouette Diamond Sweepstakes, P.O. Box 779, Madison Square Station, New York, NY 10159. Entries must be postmarked between February 1 and September 30, 1985. Silhouette is not responsible for lost, late or misdirected mail.

3. First Prize of diamond jewelry, consisting of a necklace, ring, bracelet and earrings will be awarded. Approximate retail value is $50,000 U.S./$62,500 Canadian. Second Prize of 100 Silhouette Home Reader Service Subscriptions will be awarded. Approximate retail value of each is $162.00 U.S./$180.00 Canadian. No substitution, duplication, cash redemption or transfer of prizes will be permitted. Odds of winning depend upon the number of valid entries received. One prize to a family or household. Income taxes, other taxes and insurance on First Prize are the sole responsibility of the winners.

4. Winners will be selected under the supervision of RONALD SMILEY INC., an independent judging organization whose decisions are final, by random drawings from valid entries postmarked by September 30, 1985, and receive no later than October 7, 1985. Entry in this sweepstakes indicates your awareness of the Official Rules. Winners who are residents of Canada must answer correctly a time-related arithmetical skill-testing question to qualify. First Prize winner will be notified by certified mail and must submit an Affidavit of Compliance within 10 days of notification. Returned Affidavits or prizes that are refused or undeliverable will result in alternative names being randomly drawn. Winners may be asked for use of their name and photo at no additional compensation.

5. For a First Prize winner list, send a stamped self-addressed envelope postmarked by September 30, 1985. In Canada, mail to Silhouette Diamond Contest Winner, Suite 309, 238 Davenport Road, Toronto, Ontario M5R 1J6. In the United States, mail to Silhouette Diamond Contest Winner, P.O. Box 18: Bowling Green Station, New York, NY 10274. This offer will appear in Silhouette publications and at participating retailers. Offer void in Quebec and subject to all Federal, Provincial, State and Municipal laws and regulations and wherever prohibited or restricted by law.

SDR-A-

She fought for a bold future
until she could no longer
ignore the…

TECHO OF THUNDER
MAURA SEGER

Author of **Eye of the Storm**

ECHO OF THUNDER is the love story of James
Callahan and Alexis Brockton, who forge a union
that must withstand the pressures of their own
desires and the challenge of building a new television
empire.

Author Maura Seger's writing has been described by
Romantic Times as having a "superb blend of
historical perspective, exciting romance and a deep
and abiding passion for the human soul."

**Available at your favorite
retail outlet in SEPTEMBER.**

For the woman who expects a little more out of love, get Silhouette Special Edition.

Take 4 books free—no strings attached.

If you yearn to experience more passion and pleasure in your romance reading ... to share even the most private moments of romance and sensual love between spirited heroines and their ardent lovers, then Silhouette Special Edition has everything you've been looking for.

Get 6 books each month before they are available anywhere else!

Act now and we'll send you four exciting Silhouette Special Edition romance novels. They're our gift to introduce you to our convenient home subscription service. Every month, we'll send you six new passion-filled Special Edition books. Look them over for 15 days. If you keep them, pay just $11.70 for all six. Or return them at no charge.

We'll mail your books to you *two full months before they are available* anywhere else. Plus, with every shipment, you'll receive the Silhouette Books Newsletter absolutely free. *And with Silhouette Special Edition there are never any shipping or handling charges.*

Mail the coupon today to get your four free books — and more romance than you ever bargained for.

Silhouette Special Edition is a service mark and a registered trademark.

Silhouette Desire

COMING NEXT MONTH

BEYOND LOVE—Ann Major
Nine years had passed since a misunderstanding had forced Dinah to leave Morgan Hastings. Armed with the truth, Morgan set out to win her back.

THE TENDER STRANGER—Diana Palmer
After a whirlwind romance, Dani St. Clair found herself blissfully married to a man she hardly knew. Nothing could have shattered her happiness...until his dangerous secret was revealed.

MOON MADNESS—Freda Vasilos
Two years of separation had changed nothing. Jason Stephanou was still the only man capable of driving all reason from Sophie's mind. He was the one she loved. How could she leave him again?

STARLIGHT—Penelope Wisdom
An accident suddenly ended jockey Trevor Laird's career and brought her face-to-face once again with Steven Montford, the man she had always loved, and the father of a child he didn't know existed.

YEAR OF THE POET—Ann Hurley
Child psychologist Joyce Lanier had a good head on her shoulders. Little could rattle this calm professional until wild Irish poet Neill Riorden pierced her reserve and shook her to her very core.

A BIRD IN HAND—Dixie Browning
When Anny Cousins decided to take in a boarder from the nearby university, she looked forward to playing dominoes with a stodgy old professor. She was in for a big surprise!

AVAILABLE THIS MONTH